Praise for

 WITHOUT

"Sharp and ferocious, uncompromising and funny, *Lady without Land* is a maddening and compulsively readable novel, filled to the brim with brash anecdotes and tender insights, too, about family, sex, doubt, and the search for self. Proof positive that we all have stories we read and hear, desperate to find something to drown out our sorrows, and find ourselves serving up straight shots of our own defiant music."

— MANUEL MUÑOZ, author of
What You See in the Dark, Zigzagger, and
The Faith Healer of Olive Avenue

"Vazquez's debut is exceptional. With mindblowing creativity, *Lady without Land*'s original construct of following a young Mexican woman's life via literature and cocktail recipes is a powerful cultural education that is at times heartbreaking, poetic, funny, and at all times, of the highest literary value. A perfect blend of engaging plot and prose, Vazquez is sure to make a huge name in literature—and thank the Gods of Bartenders for such intoxicating new blood!"

— SHANNON KIRK, international bestselling
author of *Method 15/33* and recipient of Literary
Classics Seal of Approval for *The Extraordinary
Journey of Vivienne Marshall*

More Praise

"By turns witty, tragic, and wholly subversive, Krystal Anali Vazquez's *Lady without Land* tracks a young Latina woman through a labyrinth of familial crises and relationship blunders, via the lens of putative book reviews and cocktail recipes. From LA to DC to, finally, New York, readers encounter this narrator's growth as she navigates the socioeconomic ladder, routing herself through government bureaucracies and academic institutions, and with them, a host of (often preventable) wreckage. Through it all, Vazquez exudes a penchant for humor and satire, marking this intelligent tome as, quite simply, a compulsively readable and wildly entertaining debut."

— JOHN JAMES, author of *The Milk Hours*

"Krystal Anali Vazquez is a mixologist; she brings together coming-of-age stories, authentic Latinx characters, and tasty drink recipes that intrigue and inspire you. Her novel transports you to Los Angeles, New York City, and rural parts of Mexico through vignettes as well as meditations on books from the Western literary canon. The book spans the protagonist's formidable years as she explores her womanhood. From her relationships with her mother and father and their adolescence, to her moments with her own siblings, and her different relationships with men and women, the protagonist bears it all to you and brings you into her mundo, a world that so many can relate to and learn from."

— CELESTE GUZMÁN MENDOZA,
author of *Beneath the Halo* and
co-founder of CantoMundo

LADY WITHOUT LAND: SEÑORITA SIN TIERRA

2023 George Garrett Fiction Prize Winner

Krystal Anali Vazquez

Selected by Manuel Muñoz

Established in 1998, The George Garrett Fiction Prize highlights one book per year for excellence in a short story collection or novel.

2022 WINNER:

Chloe Chun Seim, *Churn*
Selected by Vi Khi Nao

2021 WINNER:

J.E. Sumerau, *Transmission*
Selected by Selah Saterstrom

PAST WINNERS:

Jenny Shank, *Mixed Company*
William Black, *In the Valley of the Kings*
Susan Lowell, *Two Desperados*
Jim Kelly, *Pitchman's Blues*

See the complete list of winners & purchase their books on our website:
texasreviewpress.org

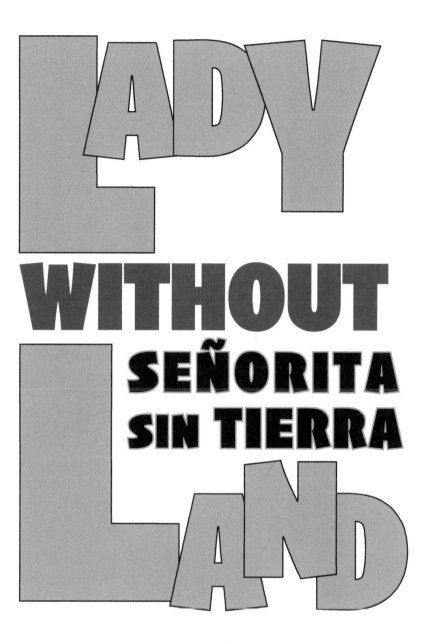

LADY WITHOUT LAND

SEÑORITA SIN TIERRA

Krystal Anali Vazquez

Winner of the 2023 George Garrett Fiction Prize
Selected by Manuel Muñoz

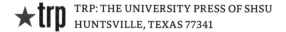

★trp TRP: THE UNIVERSITY PRESS OF SHSU
HUNTSVILLE, TEXAS 77341

Library of Congress Cataloging-in-Publication Data

Names: Vazquez, Krystal Anali, 1989- author.
Title: Lady without land / Krystal Anali Vazquez.
Other titles: Señorita sin tierra
Description: First edition. | Huntsville, Texas : TRP: The University Press
    of SHSU, [2024]
Identifiers: LCCN 2024011775 (print) | LCCN 2024011776 (ebook) | ISBN
    9781680033908 (paperback) | ISBN 9781680033915 (ebook)
Subjects: LCSH: Mexican American women--Ethnic identity--Fiction. | Mexican
    American families--Fiction. | Los Angeles (Calif.)--Fiction. | LCGFT:
    Bildungsromans. | Experimental fiction.
Classification: LCC PS3622.A9657 L33 2024 (print) | LCC PS3622.A9657
    (ebook) | DDC 813/.6--dc23/eng/20240422
LC record available at https://lccn.loc.gov/2024011775
LC ebook record available at https://lccn.loc.gov/2024011776

FIRST EDITION

Cover design by Cody Gates, Happenstance Type-O-Rama
Interior design by Maureen Forys, Happenstance Type-O-Rama
Author photo: Chrissy Connors
Cover photo: Girl-with-red-hat @ Unsplash
Printed and bound in the United States of America

TRP: The University Press of SHSU
Huntsville, Texas 77341
texasreviewpress.org

Para mi familia en la tierra
y para mi sapo en el cielo

CONTENTS

Books/Libros

Cocktails/Cócteles

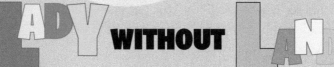ADY WITHOUT 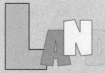AND

2 parts Mexi-can

2 parts Southern California

1 part District of Columbia

1 part Manhattan

Dash(es) Ferocious Wit

Dash(es) Cosmic Loneliness

ACHEBE, CHINUA. *THINGS FALL APART.* PRINT.

My mom has a breakdown in the kitchen, as my summer
vacation from middle school comes to an end. My older sister,
Karina, and I had been slowly waking up to the hum of her
ceiling fan when we were jolted upright by oak cabinets—banged
open and slammed—and drawers, exonerating all their contents,
thudding on the tile. We run top speed downstairs to find our
mom and see what looks like a little girl having her first tantrum;
she's beating at her chest and screaming at the top of her lungs
about "caballos y dinero"—

Because your papi, an alcoholic and a gambler, was always one for
the ponies; and your mami, an entrepreneur and a salon owner,
was always about the money. For a man who was born with
nothing in México, you always figured your papi thought he had
nothing to lose. Your mom continues sobbing uncontrollably
in Karina's breasts and neither of them sees when your father
tiptoes across the tile, makes eye contact with you, and closes the
door to the garage silently behind him, the portrait of Jesus next
to the door shedding a tear.

BLACK AND BLUE SEÑORITA

Gather the following for your shooters:
1½ oz. Tequila
½ oz. Black Raspberry Liqueur
½ oz. Blue Curacao
3 oz. Sour Mix
1 oz. Sprite
Shake with Ice.
Strain into shot glasses.

I am 23 years old and find my mother bruised all over her face and stomach, using a walker years before her time.

She's doubled over and carefully eating oatmeal at a rickety garden table my father set up for her in their master bedroom, because she can't get downstairs. My father expects me to take care of her as she heals from the plastic surgery they drove to Tijuana for, take care of her after all the years he's told her she wasn't "flaca" like the stars in his telenovelas and how he didn't ever want her to look "acabada." They both lied and said my father was taking my mom on a vacation for her birthday. I scream words in Spanish I didn't even know I knew. She's the only one bringing in money. He's unemployed. She was beautiful the way she was. My father banishes me from the kingdom, and I go sleep on my sister and brother-in-law's black leather couch for a month.[1]

---

[1] To see how Mexican daughters are "supposed" to take care of their parents, *see* **"Esquivel, Laura,"** and for more on the black leather couch, *sip* **"¿Is that a Banana in Your Pocket?"**

ALLENDE, ISABEL. *THE HOUSE OF THE SPIRITS / LA CASA DE LOS ESPÍRITUS.* PRINT.

Mariachi Guadalajara came to us by van. Up the hill they drove, on our quiet little suburban street, to wake us up before dawn. My parents called them to play on my older sister's 15th birthday, her quinceañera. My parents didn't care that it was a school night. My parents didn't care that we lived in a virtually all-white neighborhood. My parents didn't care how much a serenade en la madrugada would cost them. All they cared about was that their first daughter, Karina the Beautiful, hear las mañanitas on that September day that marked her entry into this world. I sat on the stairs in my footie pajamas and watched her cry tears of joy as they sang her canción after canción and when the squad of sleepy-eyed white men in bathroom robes came to the front door, confused by the violin-vihuela-trumpet-guitarrón-guitarra-de-golpe alarm clock, my parents, somehow, made them all disappear.

BEETLEJUICE

In a Double Old-Fashioned glass with Ice, pour:
1 oz. Vodka
½ oz. Yellow Melon Liqueur
½ oz. Blue Curacao
¼ oz. Raspberry Schnapps
2 oz. Sweet and Sour
Twist on a stick (for the sandworm factor) a Cucumber Ribbon.
Stir drink with it until the juice is loose.
Serve with a black-and-white striped straw.

I am 5 years old and on my first family roadtrip from Los Angeles, California to Tenamaxtlán, Jalisco. My older sister, Karina, decides to carry the torch and bully me the entire way, like our brother Nacho did to her in the past.

At home, she pins me to the floor and bungee-jumps saliva down an inch from my little, squishy face and back into her mouth. In the car, she holds all my stuffed animals hostage. At home, she knows I learned about Bloody Mary from other kids in kindergarten and she's made me terrified of the bathroom. In the car, she points to all the indias with the trenzas on the side of the road and tells me those ladies are my real familia. At home, she turns me into her little slave—getting her fluffier pillows, making her chocolate "Quick" or orange "Tang," and changing the channel to *The Real World* or *90210* for her—all so that she won't say: "Beetlejuice, Beetlejuice, BEETLE—"and make *him* appear.

And in the car, she dangles my favorite stuffed animal, a parrot named Pancho, out of the window somewhere in Sinaloa. With a bump he flies into the jungle, and our father refuses to turn the car around.

AUSTEN, JANE. *PRIDE AND PREJUDICE.* PRINT.

A present on my 13th birthday from an older sister who rarely reads but knows *I* love to, though I could barely get through the opening chapter the first time I opened the book. By 17, I was using it for my high school "thesis" and by 21, I was using it on the most literary one-night-stand-of-British-descent I've ever had: "Well, it *is* a truth universally acknowledged that a single man in possession of a beach house must not be in want of a girlfriend," I said, as I searched for my bra and lace panties.

ADIOS MOTHERFUCKER

Pour into a very tall Highball glass filled with Ice:
½ oz. Hayman's London Dry Gin
½ oz. Light Rum
½ oz. Patrón Silver Blanco Tequila
½ oz. Ketel One Vodka
½ oz. Blue Curacao Liqueur
2 oz. Sweet & Sour Mix
2 oz. Sprite
Garnish with plenty of sour Lemon Slices.

I am almost 25 years old. Enrique flies across the country to see me and "accidentally" calls me his ex-girlfriend's name in Washington, DC, my brand-new city.

He's scheduled to stay for a week, but we can barely get through the third day. On the fourth day, he tells me he'll leave if I don't stop acting like a bitch. I roll my eyes and jump in the shower without a word.

When I get out, I find all his button-downs and white undershirts are gone and he's erased his number and all our messages from my phone. I sit on the uneven air mattress we popped the night before in missionary and I don't even bother drying my dripping wet hair.[2]

....
[2] *Pair also with* **"Absolut La La Land."**

BECKETT, SAMUEL. *WAITING FOR GODOT.* PRINT.

As a priest rubs ash on your little forehead with his rough thumb, so begins the season of waiting in long lines and staring at bible stories told by stained glass.

That March, your mom prefers going to the church in San Fernando instead of going to the one near your house because there are more Masses en español there. You like this one too, because there's a huge mural of Jesus walking out of sunset clouds, and your mom will buy you elote and raspados when you get out. After watching *Looney Tunes* all morning while your mother and sister get ready upstairs, they emerge fresh from their cloud of Sunday hair spray. You get to church and ask your teenage sister why all the statues and portraits, and even the huge mural of Jesus, are covered completely in purple cloth. She tells you it's because on Easter Sunday there's a huge light show in the church and a 3D Jesus comes out of the wall and walks down the aisle and talks to people. Even shakes a few hands.

But Easter comes and goes that year, and the next, and no 3D Jesus. You figure it's because your family went to Mass at the wrong time.

THREE WISE MEN & A DIRTY MEXICAN (SHOOTER)

Add the following 3 whiskeys to a shaker filled with Ice:
½ oz. Jack Daniel's 10 Years Old Tennessee Whiskey
½ oz. Jim Beam Black Kentucky Bourbon Whiskey
½ oz. Johnnie Walker Black Label Scotch Whiskey
Shake & Strain into one shot glass.
Top off with Jose Cuervo Tequila and Shoot.

I am 21 years old and one of my dad's female coworkers comes to our house to give him a Christmas present as a "thank-you for all his hard work" at the banquet hall.

She's standing there with her husband and two sons behind her. Our "dollhouse," as we liked to call it, always looked so pretty during Christmastime. My mom would hire "Handy Manny" to string icicles on the outside and I would decorate the tree that rotated and spun in the foyer. My dad's coworker tells him that the house is beautiful and Dad thanks her, stringing together some other words in English.

She says they got lost on the way and were just *sooo* surprised that he lived in such a big house. [3]

---

[3] For more on what she might actually mean, *gulp* **"Pink Beaner,"** and *sip* **"Dirty Mexican Lemonade."**

BORGES, JORGE LUIS. *THE GARDEN OF FORKING PATHS / EL JARDÍN DE SENDEROS QUE SE BIFURCAN.* PRINT.

In college you read Gilles Deleuze to make sense of Borges and it crystallizes but does not quite cement.

In graduate school you start to collect: recollection-images; dream-images; time-images; and movement-images. Opsigns and sonsigns. And hyalosigns. And chronosigns. And noo signs and lectosigns. The positive and the predictable. Making. Remaking. Unmaking. Placement. Displacement. Acting. Re-enacting. Moving horizons. Decentered centers. Translations into different times. Different places. Lost, but found, in all the difference and repetition.

THE REVOLVER

In a mixing glass filled with Ice, pour:
2 oz. Bulleit Bourbon
½ oz. Tia Maria Coffee Liqueur
2 Dashes Angostura Orange Bitters
Strain into a chilled Manhattan glass.
Hold a lit match near the drink's surface.
Against the lip, squeeze a strip (skin-side-out) of Orange Peel.
Express its oils through the flame and garnish with the Flamed Peel.

I am 7 years old and my Dad is screaming for his pistolas.

You get out of bed to see your Dad in his white Charro shirt with dark-brown embroidery, the same one he had worn to a family wedding earlier in the evening, now paired with just his tighty whities. The last you remember he was taking Tequila shots and he must have lost count. And now it's 2 o'clock in the morning and he's running up and down the stairs of this suburban home, demanding that your mom and your sister Karina give him his guns, and he's searching the entire house for them, ravaging every drawer and every closet. The guns he bought in Mexico. They're *his* guns and he *needs* his guns.

"Why do you want them now?" your mom screams. "You could shoot us accidentally in the back or leg, and what's the point of that?"

Before he runs into the backyard to search there, he screams into the night: "I just *need* them. They're *mine!*"[4]

. . . .
[4] Years later when you asked Karina if this had simply been a dream—she said your mom had given *her* your dad's pistolas, "for safekeeping," when Karina was 16—she kept them for years in a backpack under her bed, hidden behind old toys.

BRONTË, CHARLOTTE. *JANE EYRE.* PRINT.

"Jane is able to choose Mr. Rochester because he loses his sight," your classmate tells you. You had read this book before coming to graduate school, but never with this lens. "Once the master of Thornfield Hall becomes 'crippled,' he and Jane are equals," she explains. You nod and think back to the young man you've been dating on and off again for the past few months, the one who needs his cane to stay up on dates in The District. The handsome late-twenty-something Virginia gentleman with the bright blue eyes and the multiple sclerosis. Later, after you finish grading your students' papers, you consider how you and he know how it feels to walk in an unfair world. That night when you see him in his Woodley Park apartment, his privilege slowly melts off you and into the mattress.

LORD AND LADY

1½ oz. Dakabend Dark Rum
½ oz. Tia Maria
Pour ingredients into an Old-Fashioned glass
almost filled with Ice Cubes
Garnish with a sprig of Mint.

I am 25 years old and fly back to Los Angeles to visit my boyfriend—my second Mexican boyfriend, Enrique. We forgave each other only to be here again.

"You're a fucking liar," he roars into my face. "Your dad could read! You need to read to get a business license!" He has me backed up against his bedroom door in Los Feliz. I threaten to leave, and he bites my cheek. Hard.

He had asked to see your personal statement. The one that got you a cushy full ride to graduate school. The one about how your dad can't read or write. In between tears, you tell him your mom is the one with the business. *She* can read. You never said *she* couldn't read.
"But even then, she always needs some help."
Still, he keeps calling you a liar. Screams, "You don't deserve it!"
You run out of his house and into your car.
He's the one whose mom smuggled him across the border!
You nearly hit him with your car after he jumps in front of it.
He's the one who was actually born in Mexico!
He slams his hands on the hood. *He's* DACA.
You hop out of the car and start crying on the ground in the middle of the street with the engine running.
He calls you a fucking psycho and leaves you there.

BUKOWSKI, CHARLES. *WOMEN.* PRINT.

You've always felt something strong for dirty old men and at 17 you were absolutely in love with this lowlife. At 23, you are re-reading *Women* during your lunch break to see if you still feel something. The hot Korean girl and her Indian sidekick are on a juice cleanse that week and look absolutely feeble during the 9 to 5. When you get home, you mention this to your mother while making a quesadilla, telling her that you personally prefer a little meat on your women. She screams: "why do you have to say '*my* women'? Why can't you just say '*women*'?"

You fall to the kitchen tile in a fit of laughter as your father snores on the couch and the music from his telenovela replaces the pregnant pause in kitchen.

"You're scaring me," your mother screams.

"Mom, do you know how many men I've slept with?" you manage to spit out while grasping your side.

"You're scaring me," your mother screams.

ABSOLUT LA LA LAND

1½ oz. Absolut Los Angeles Vodka
1 oz. Cranberry Juice
1 oz. Lemon-Lime Soda
1 oz. Pomegranate Juice
Build up ingredients in a Highball glass over Ice.
Top with a long twist of Lime.

I am 24 years old and I ride my coworker in the backseat of his car after a night of heavy drinking in West Hollywood.

We both have had too many cocktails at my going-away party and that leads to a blowjob in the office and then to him bending me over the hood of his car in the parking garage.[5] I've been training him for the past two weeks on how to take over my paralegal job at the firm.

When I am done, I notice he wears the same plain white t-shirts underneath his dress shirt as my dad. Maybe it's a Mexican thing? "That was great, but I have to go," I tell him. Jeans around his ankles, he begins to follow me to my car and asks me if I want to get pancakes at a nearby diner and then have seconds. I tell him it's late and I have to get home. "Besides, you're still digesting firsts," I say. I get home and find my dad on the couch, waiting up for me at 2 o'clock in the morning. He asks me where I've been. He was worried. "Fui a verlas porque ellas no vienen," I say. He smiles and I give him a big hug and a kiss before I go upstairs to bed.[6]

....

[5] To this day, you wonder if there's security footage of you in that compromising position.

[6] *Pair also with* **"Adios Motherfucker"** *and* **"Horse and Jockey."**

BURGESS, ANTHONY. A CLOCKWORK ORANGE. PRINT & FILM.

On the wall of The Handsome Italian's bedroom is a brain in a bowler hat hovering above a juicer and the words "La Naranja Mecánica."

"I acquired that bit of art in Cuba," he says. "I quite like it," he adds, and you notice he says "quite," quite a bit. His UES apartment is unlike anything you have ever seen. Though you have lived in NYC for a year and half, you rarely leave the school accommodations on the west side, and you have never actually been in a residential building with a doorman, a view of the park, and nannies exclusively taking kids to school in the morning (you'll see that in the morning). Everything in that apartment is sophisticated like The Handsome Italian, in his early 50s, who owns it—ceramic bowls from Turkey he serves you decadent ice cream in; expensive red wine from none other than Italy; a drawer full of sex toys that will take away your voice for hours to come; cashmere blankets, handloomed in Nepal, he wraps you in after; and a plushy sapphire-colored robe that frames his long chestnut hair and the wide grin he reserves for you, all the better.

On your frosty February date earlier that night, over ramen and Hot Toddies, the song "Singin' in the Rain" came up in conversation. You make a comment about how the song reflected an optimistic post-World War II society in the 1950s film, but by the 1970s disillusionment set in, as evidenced by that same song being used in Kubrick's famous rape scene, at least that is what you learned in your college film course. Moments before you fall asleep in The Handsome Italian's arms, he whispers in your ear that it was *that* moment at the table he realized he wanted to bring you home with him.[7]

....

[7] For more on one of the best first dates on record, *see* **"Homer,"** and for more on amorous times between you and The Handsome Italian, *sip* **"Greek Sex on the Beach."**

DROOG'S DATE COCKTAIL

Shake well with Ice:
1½ oz East London White Rum
2 tsp. Cherry Brandy
2 tsp Bols or DeKuyper Triple Sec
Strain into Martini glass filled with Lime Wheels.
Dangle lip with Cherries.

I am 6 years old and I see my older sister Karina and my prima Lizette jump into the bed of a dusty pickup truck to join a bunch of gangsters from Compton and Inglewood. The bald gangsters will be taking them to the bullfight at the edge of the pueblo.

You and your papi have poked your heads out from crumbling adobe walls to see them go in a very 90s scene—short jean miniskirts, white platform heels, burgundy lips and all—lost in a half ton load of at least ten teenage boys drowning in knee-length white shirts. You have made your yearly pilgrimage[8] to the pueblo in Mexico and instead of being courted by the local charros of Tenamaxtlán and Atengo, who whirl their way so effortlessly through ropes, your sister and prima opt for the Cali crew. Your papi is wearing the Stetson you are never allowed to touch and his cream cowboy suit from Jim's Western Wear that your mom bought him in San Fernando. Your papi tells you he does not understand what your teenage sister sees "en esos pelones feos." You giggle and tell your Papi he's your date to the bullfight and esos pelones are not your type. He calls you his little sopito, scoops you into his arms, and kisses you on your chubby cheek. You twirl the ends of his bolo tie in your small hands and lightly whip them against his heart, giving him a huge flash of your milk-tooth grin.[9]

---

[8] *See also* **"Chaucer, Geoffrey"** and *pair with* **"Border Crossing."**

[9] For more on milk teeth, *sip* **"Milk Tooth."**

CALVINO, ITALO. *IF ON A WINTER'S NIGHT A TRAVELER.* PRINT.

. . . pushes you. Like full-on shoves you onto a 1 train—

The last train was jam-packed, and there is no way you're maneuvering yourself between all that pissed-off flesh. So, you wait for the next train and, anxious to get back to your apartment uptown, you are determined to fit on it. But the woman lined up behind you on the platform is even more determined. When the doors open, and you do the customary subway shuffle, you feel her dig her nails deep into your arms and drive you into the innards of the subway car. You've been pushed before but this is simply egregious. You had a wretched day studying torts in a library downtown and had just brainstormed an image for a story you'd like to write (to forget the day) when you get home. But the woman knocks it out of you. The image falls straight into the detritus of the subway track below, a rat probably now paddling through the infested waters of your thoughts . . .

—you hear a voice at full blast: "YO, DON'T PUSH ME." You tend to be the quietest person in a room and rarely say "yo" so you doubt it could be you. *But it is you.* You can tell because a few other New Yorkers look over at you and give you a simple nod of understanding.

GENT OF THE JURY

In a mixing glass ½ filled with Ice:
2 oz. Gin
1½ tsp. Dry Vermouth
Stir well. Strain into short cocktail glass.
Garnish with 7 Cocktail Onions.

I am 27 years old and worry these stories I am working on when I need a break from law school are a form of copyright infringement.

Is Jose Cuervo or Jack Daniels going to sue me for using their product, in relevant part, to tell a story about squirting? Will the cocktail app on my iPhone that I have been poring over (and *pouring* over), take issue with the fact that I am using their compilation of recipes for my passion project? I fall asleep pondering these thoughts. They almost have a chilling effect, and I consider scrapping the project altogether.[10] Being both a "bard" and "barrister" can be someone else's reality. Then I hear my answer during Property class when the professor goes over *Feist Publications, Inc. v. Rural Telephone Service Co.*, 499 U.S. 340 (1991). There, the court clarified that the intent of copyright law was not, as claimed by Rural and some lower courts, to reward the efforts of persons collecting information—the so-called "sweat of the brow" or "industrious collection" doctrine—but rather "to promote the Progress of Science and useful Arts" (U.S. Const. art. I, § 8, cl. 8). That is, to encourage creative expression.

So that's it then. The cocktail app is clearly not being creative by merely collecting cocktail recipes, and as long as I'm creating these stories with some "modicum of creativity" then all is well. But are they created with some "modicum of creativity"? Well, ladies and gentlemen of the jury—that's for you to decide.

....

[10] For more on the meta-textual and what it means to give yourself up to the writing process, *see* **"Calvino, Italo,"** *supra* and *see also* **"Unamuno, Miguel"** *infra.*

CARROLL, LEWIS. ALICE'S ADVENTURES IN WONDERLAND. PRINT.

While procrastinating on a paper for your Morrison seminar, you come across a meme. It features Alice, with a cat at her feet, consoling Dorothy, with her head in her hands and Toto in her lap. *I've seen some shit*, the meme reads.

And you've seen some shit in your childhood, too.

With parents who worked all day and an older sister who didn't mind what you watched; you've seen some shit. You remember watching that Aerosmith video with Alicia Silverstone and Liv Tyler, and the way it excited you, somehow. You remember watching a lot of *The Crush* and *Poison Ivy* in '95, more than any first grader should. You even saw *Poison Ivy* dubbed in Spanish with your sister, while vacationing in a hotel in Ensenada, when your parents were out to dinner.

In fourth grade, your sister had to watch *Psycho* for her freshman film class so you watched that too—and at a friend's birthday party the same year, the birthday girl wanted to watch Stephen King's *IT*, so you did. After *that* double feature, getting into the shower was almost impossible.

EYES WIDE SHUT

½ oz. Southern Comfort
½ oz. Crown Royal
½ oz. Amaretto
½ oz. Orange Juice
½ oz. Pineapple Juice
½ oz. Cranberry Juice
1 splash of Grenadine Syrup
Shake and pour into a chilled Martini glass.

I am 11 years old, and my mom asks what I think my older brother spends all his money on. "He must be making almost $300,000 a year selling all those cars—so where does it go?"

"I bet it's strippers and cocaine," you tell your mom. She's shocked that's where your mind went. But when you imagine your 25-year-old brother's life, you envision *American Psycho* meets *Eyes Wide Shut*, the former, he told you, was one of his favorite movies. And when you're living in New York City for law school in your late 20s, you call your parents and ask them about their recent trip to Puerto Vallarta with your brother. Apparently, your brother Nacho paid for everything—the hotel, the plane ride, the food, and even the renovations for your parent's house in Tenamaxtlán. And your sister had already told you that your brother brought his "girlfriend" and left his second wife and son, William, at home in Los Angeles. Curious, you ask your mom about the mystery girlfriend.

"We try not to ask too many questions," your mother says.

CATHER, WILLA. *DEATH COMES FOR THE ARCHBISHOP.* PRINT.

Saturday mornings are the hardest. It was on a Saturday morning when your daddy cut up the meat for the wedding he was catering that day, left your mami her breakfast and lunch (lovingly packaged and still warm on the kitchen counter, como siempre), and sat down to rest in his favorite livingroom chair. The one with your first-communion portrait so cruelly positioned above—9-year-old you, cradling a crucifix in your little arms—while your father's heart slowly dims below. Meanwhile, you're kicking ass in kickboxing class off Broadway. When you collapse sweaty in the street, New Yorkers, some from the kickboxing class and others passing by, will pick you up.

You didn't really need your older brother Nacho to tell you he was gone, to know. Your mother's voicemails—a broken, wailing pitch, screaming to call her back—told you she had lost her husband of 44 years. Paramedics came and tried to save what was already lost. Your brother punched the kitchen cabinet—a sizable crack still remains. Your mother cries that your papi only complained of heartburn a few days before. Only heartburn. He said he couldn't burp, that's all. Because it was Memorial Day Weekend, it took hours for the coroner to come. Your family covered him in a cobija, waiting and praying together. The people came to pick up the food for their catered wedding, your daddy's body still sprawled out on the floor of the living room. Your sister tells you this on the phone that afternoon. You don't want to book the plane back to California right away. Because when you book it, it will mean the only man who ever truly loved you really is gone.

MORTUARY MIX

In a pitcher ¼ full of Ice:
Add 1 bottle or 25 oz of Tom Collins Mix
and 8 oz (or more) of Everclear Grain Alcohol.

I am 28 years old and I cannot take my eyes off my father's hands, hands that are positively frozen.[11]

Those are the hands that cooked me delicious food, hands that held me, hands that held mine every night he would come to my room to wish me goodnight at 9pm (so he could make his 6am shift). And yet, those hands that held me now look something closer to The Penguin's chilled and deformed meat hooks from the 1992 Tim Burton *Batman Returns* movie—something that might make me laugh if it weren't the most horrific thing I have ever seen. I thought I knew what it meant to die but the details fill in and erase the old concept: how when the viewing takes place two weeks after the passing, what remains of my father's left thumb is blackened underneath, staged for me not to notice, but it's almost all I can see. Once the rosary and viewing are over and my entire extended family trickles out—all except my immediate family—the funeral director of "Eternal Valley" asks if we want to watch the lid close. When it shuts forever with an eerie echo no one knows what to say. I touch the wood with my palm and speak first: "Goodnight, Daddy" and step back. My older brother and sister follow my lead.

When it is time to go, we all use *our* hands to make sure our mom is able to walk to the exit of the chapel upright.

. . . .

[11] For more on his hands, *also sip* **"Working Man's Zinfandel."**

CERVANTES, MIGUEL DE. *DON QUIXOTE.* PRINT.

From kindergarten to second grade, I was the Doña of the
playground, and she was my Sancho Panza. Together we turned
swing sets into dragons, and jungle gyms into our castles. In
third grade however, my favorite little red-haired girl moved
to the third-grade classroom far across the playground. Worlds
apart, she befriended some other brunette named Nadia Nazem.
I could see them as tiny specks, side by side on the swings. My
Sancho Panza had found a Sancha in my La Mancha.

SANCHO PANZA

2 oz. Cream Sherry
¾ oz. Campari
1 dash Angostura Bitters
Stir and serve neat in a Copita glass.

I am 23 years old and I am dancing seductively in the kitchen with my best friend from elementary school, Cynthia.[12]

We turn the center granite island into a stage and open and close the refrigerator doors, flashing our breasts for the leftover beans, rice, and carne asada, our audience. My parents are sleeping upstairs. At least I hope so because two bottles of liquor in, she removes her clothing: her bra and pajamas pants plop on the tile. I notice her copper embers curling sweetly. I look up, smile, and tell her she has just the right amount of meat on her body.

[12] For more tales from the kitchen, *see* **"Bukowski, Charles."**

CHAUCER, GEOFFREY. *THE CANTERBURY TALES.* PRINT.

Every year your family makes the pilgrimage.[13] Once you get to México, the excursions begin: the three-hour walk to the next pueblo and a five-minute crawl down the church aisle on your knees to see the Virgen de Atengo; the two-hour drive through the most serpentine mountain road that it always ends in both a visit to the Virgen de Talpa[14] and a plastic bag full of your mother's vomit; and the five-minute walk to the town square for the most delicious, thick, deep-fried churros, wrapped in butcher paper, you've ever had. That year your mother has allowed your older sister's boyfriend/future-husband, Carlos, to come to your grandparents' house in México, but he has to sleep on the floor. You and your sister sleep in the bed. On the last night in México your parents are at a party and you're trying to fall asleep. But your sister and her boyfriend won't stop talking about how churros would really hit the spot. So, they give you a few pesos and when you come back with the deep-fried goodness, they look *very* happy.[15]

. . . .

[13] *See also* **"Steinbeck, John."**

[14] For more on the Virgen de Talpa, *sip* **"Immaculada."**

[15] Years later, Karina and Carlos will tell you they wanted you to leave so they could fuck. It's so obvious now.

¿IS THAT A BANANA IN YOUR POCKET?

Fill a Collins glass with:
Ice Cubes
2 parts Whiskey
1 part Banana Liqueur
2 parts Sweet and Sour

I am 23 years old and I am volun-told to babysit my nephew,
Victor, because my older sister Karina and her husband,
Carlos, never really get to have "date night."

But it's no problem because you love that little "chili-bean." Half Mexican
and half Chilean, his laugh sounds like the warmth of Mexican Abuelita
hot chocolate and his eyebrows hill over like Andean vineyards, like his
father's. After Victor falls asleep you rest on their black leather couch
where you're woken up at 3am by the Latino equivalent of Scott and
Zelda Fitzgerald—booze, flapper-length dress and all—your sister goes
to the bathroom to take off her makeup and you try to get back to sleep
when Victor's father spoons you from behind in the darkness. You pretend
to be asleep, hoping he'll go away, but soon your sister saves you with a
scream to her husband: "What are you doing to my sister? GET OFF my
sister." And over morning eggs and sausage from McDonald's (as their
"thank you,") you're convinced the night wiped their memories clean.[16]

....
[16] For more spooning, *also sip* **"Miscarriage."**

CHOPIN, KATE. *THE AWAKENING.* PRINT.

The Editor dumps you three days after your 26th birthday and three weeks before you have to go to a friend's wedding in Jekyll Island, Georgia. Even when they played the Seu Jorge cover of "Life on Mars" at the reception, you held it together, even though Bowie songs make you think of him. But by the time you all get back to the beach house that night, you begin to guzzle red wine out of the bottle like it's Gatorade. It makes you sprint to skinny-dip in the Atlantic, even after the plan had long been vetoed out of fear a stray jellyfish might sting your vulvas. You leave your fancy clothes behind as breadcrumbs so your friends from graduate school can find you. It's October, it's dark, and no one is on the beach. You feel baptized and blessed and Chopin comes alive for you: there's a moment where you realize you could keep swimming and never turn around. Back on the shoreline, your friends are angry. You could have drowned. You take the towel and tell them it may have looked like you could have drowned "but they were your anchors on the beach from way out there."[17]

---

[17] But no worries—you'll get back together in a few months. *Sip* **"Bloated Bag of Monkey Spunk"** or **"Cold War."** But then, of course, you'll break up for good in a few years. *See also* **"Waugh, Evelyn."**

WET DREAM

Mix together:
½ oz. Amaretto
¼ oz. Blue Curacao
¼ oz. Crème de Banane
¼ oz. Sweet and Sour
Splash of Pineapple juice.
Chill and strain into a Martini Glass.
Through this pale blue layer:
Float ¼ oz Chambord Raspberry Liqueur
to the bottom of the glass.

I am 25 years old and meet my boyfriend's ex-girlfriend, only minutes before she goes on the burlesque stage.

She and The Editor remain good friends, and you were in the mood for burlesque, so you thought you'd kill two birds. Her stage name is "Glitter" and she's performing at Freddie's, the gay bar in Crystal City. She's dressed in a nautical-themed outfit with a sailor hat that's covered in sequins and so much glitter. A song about playing with a "dinghy" comes on and she tugs at each finger of her navy-blue gloves with her teeth. After she's done, she comes over in pasties to talk to you and The Editor. And because The Editor is twelve years older than you, you convince yourself that this is obviously what adult relationships look like. She leaves with her boyfriend, and you drink more Wet Dreams than you mean to. You bite your boyfriend's cheek when he's mid-sentence. You try to apologize with a kiss, but he pushes you away. He doesn't have the same pain threshold you do.[18]

....

[18] For more cheek-biting, *also sip* some **"Lord and Lady."**

CISNEROS, SANDRA. *THE HOUSE ON MANGO STREET / LA CASA EN MANGO STREET.* PRINT.

She's the one you came to see at the Festival of Books in Downtown Los Angeles. You heard Diego Luna read an excerpt from a children's graphic novel earlier that morning (which was incredible), but her's is the main event. On stage she mentions that she recently found a journal entry she wrote at age 30. Her 60-year-old self makes fun of her 30-year-old self, mock-scribbling in the air: "I can't imagine being anything other than a writer. That would be the best job in the world." You remember telling your parents those exact same words at age 17. From 7 to 17 you wanted to be a lawyer, but after reading this book you thought there was a chance you could be a writer. After Sandra's done mocking herself, she laughs and says she can now imagine being many things other than a writer: "I could have been a judge on *RuPaul's Drag Race*." The crowd laughs and, as if your early 20s are not hard enough, you'll wonder if it's not too late to go to law school after all.[19]

---

[19] And you do, eventually, go to law school. For the tale of the trial *see* **"Kafka, Franz."**

PINK BEANER

In a beer mug ¾ full of Crushed Ice:
3 oz. El Tesoro Tequila
8 oz. Pineapple-coconut juice, or nectar (Kern's)
1 Splash Grenadine
Stir until pink.

I am 6 years old and live in a two-story khaki-colored house with trim the color of shit.

The house is the color of your family's skin, which clashes with the eggshell and blue shades of the other houses in the neighborhood. Your mom hires "Handy Manny" to give the house a splash of color. When "Handy Manny" (who is eggshell with baby blue trim himself) learns your mother's favorite shade, he gets to work. It's not your favorite but you get used to it. Months later, your older brother comes home from the Marine Corps base in North Carolina where he's been stationed the last year. You see his friend's car pull into the driveway and run outside to hug him but he's not even looking at you. The color drains out of his face and he rushes inside to find your mother.
"FUCKING PINK WITH AVOCADO GREEN TRIM?!
As if everyone in the neighborhood didn't already fucking know we are fucking BEANERS; you do this shit to the house?!"

Your mother pleads with him, "Pero mijo—Handy Manny thought it would be such a good color."[20]

. . . .

[20] For more tales of what it's like to be brown in the white suburbs, *sip* **"Dirty Mexican Lemonade."**

CONRAD, JOSEPH. *HEART OF DARKNESS.* PRINT.

"Ven a ver los moretones que le di a tu madre," your father told you. And he chuckled over the phone because that was his humor. But you saw nothing funny about the bruises on your mother's face that looked like hard stones trailing down from her eyes to her stomach.[21] So dark, they made you stay away for a month. When you come back to confront your mother, her eyes are *still* black. And the horror struck you even deeper. At first, you're calm.

Three months before, she told you she needed to cancel your private health insurance, which she'd been paying for, because she couldn't afford it anymore, and you weren't making much at your job those days either, so you told her to terminate it, even though that left you with nothing. And you understood now.

"So, I could get hit by a car and have no health insurance to help me, could die any moment, but you have a flat stomach and pulled-back face, and that's all that matters!" you scream.

She tells you it's a business investment. It's her job to make people beautiful and no one will trust her to do that if she looks acabada. She put it on her credit card and it's her money, anyway. Like a child, she repeats in English, "*it's my money.* "It's my money, it's my money. It's my money, it's my money, it's my money."

....
[21] *Also sip* **"Black and Blue Señorita."**

DARK'N DIRTY

1 oz. Newfoundland Screech Dark Rum (Red)
4 oz. Coca-Cola
Mix and serve over Ice.

I am 16 years old wearing a penis party hat, stealing Dark Rum and Coke from my sister's bachelorette party, and stuffing tiny bottles of Kahlua into my childhood friend's bras in the dark garage, while the male stripper distracts everyone else.

Your mother doesn't like the man your sister is marrying. He's not handsome enough for her Karina the Beautiful.[22] Still, your mom was adamant that the bachelorette party be at your house, and not at Karina's future in-laws's, who know how to throw a hell of party, because it *looks* better to have it *here*. You go off to drink with your childhood friends and senior high school boys on a mountaintop, still wearing the penis party hats. When you come back, you hear the second male stripper was kind of an ass, and your mother wouldn't stop sweeping up behind the mess the strippers and partygoers made. Your sister tells you she found it embarrassing, the way the broom brushed up on people's feet during the party. You watch Karina fit her buxom bosom into the lacy-lingerie outfits she got from Frederick's and Victoria's Secret. Tipsy and tired, you sit on her bed and fork into what remains of the stripper-shaped cake's six pack to cushion the coming hangover.

....

[22] *See also* **"Allende, Isabel."**

COOPER, JAMES FENIMORE. *THE LAST OF THE MOHICANS*. PRINT.

The Editor calls you a "conquistadora" because you are extraordinarily skilled with navigation.[23] You love maps and love knowing exactly where you are and where you are going. You tell him you attribute this quality to your father's remarkable sense of direction and, most likely, the Spanish blood bubbling beneath in your Aztec veins. One Christmas, The Editor gives you a tube you can spit in with a note: *Let's see how much of a conquistadora you are.* When you get the results, you call your mom in California: "41% Iberian Peninsula—that means Spain, mami."

"Makes sense . . . my abuelo was from Spain," she says.

"You never told me that!—and 27% Native American: Western & Central Mexico—which includes Jalisco and Guanajuato, mami, so that means we are only really 27% Mexican if you really think about it; 16% Europe/South—that means Greek and Italian!"

Your DNA is basically the greatest hits of colonialism, and you try to play the rest of your results to your mother, but your father, who was listening on speaker, hijacks the phone and tells you: "ni madres—somos *Mexican* y ya."

. . . .

[23] For more on The Editor, *see also* **"Hurston, Zora Neale"** or **"Kundera, Milan"** or **"London, Jack"** or *take a gulp of* **"Cold War."**

HORNY MOHICAN

20 ml Banana Liqueur
20 ml Bailey's Irish Cream
20 ml Malibu Rum
Free Pour each ingredient into a long test tube and Shoot.

I am 28 years old and a 60+ hombre I barely know is telling me at 3am that he may have "accidentally" taken a little blue pill. This is only minutes after I wake up in the back seat of his car on an empty side street of Guadalajara and my groggy mind can barely handle it.

At Christmas, I had flown alone from the East Coast to Guadalajara. And the small pueblo my parents are from is a two-hour drive from the airport. To make my return flight, I agree to have gold-toothed Chuy, one of my dad's acquaintances, drive me from Tenamaxtlán to Guadalajara (GDL), after my parents' plane back to Los Angeles had been rescheduled (thanks, Volaris). I've seen my dad make the trip to GDL too many times, and he's looking older these days, so I say, "I am a big girl and can go alone with the old hombre."

He picks me up at midnight to make the 6am flight. After I hug my parents adiós, Chuy lets me nap on a bumpy ride to GDL.[24] When I wake up he gives me the option: airport now or "sleep" for another trienta minutos. I choose airport, and on the short ride, he says he watched me while I was sleeping and noticed how beautiful I am, not unlike my sister. Then he says it was dark while he was driving and he may have grabbed the wrong pill from a Ziplock bag. I play tonta, even though yo entiendo what he wants.

Weeks later, when the shock and fear of that night begin to fade, I recount the story to my mom. She'll say: "Well, I'm glad you didn't . . . because it's a small pueblo y la gente habla."

. . . .
[24] This will be the last time you ever hug your dad adiós. *See also* **"Cather, Willa"** or *slowly sip* **"Mortuary Mix."**

CORTÁZAR, JULIO. *HOPSCOTCH / RAYUELA.* PRINT.

In the late 1980's, on a playground in the San Fernando Valley, Karina throws her stone and makes her own rules.[25] Balancing on her left foot while wearing a yellow dress with white, Mary Jane, patent-leather shoes, she prepares to jump. She also has those white socks with frilly lace ruffling over her ankles that our mom always dressed us in at that age. She leaps and lands on "1" then "2" then skips over the stone at "3" to stand firmly on both feet at "4" and "5" before she springs to complete the sequence the way she wants. Landing within the chalky confines of "10," she stops, suspended in time. It is then that Miguel, a boy from her fifth-grade class who has been watching her from across the playground, runs up to her, places both hands on her chest and screams into her face, "Are those real?!" before running away.

After you turn 18, even though you were only a baby when this happened to Karina, you'll conjure in your mind this moment she shared with you, whenever your mother constantly asks, "Don't you want big, beautiful breasts like Karina's? Maybe we can go to Tijuana to get them done."[26]

"Actually, I don't, Mom. I really don't."

---

[25] This was a few years before our family traded San Fernando for Santa Clarita. *Pair with* **"Dirty Mexican Lemonade."**

[26] For more on the wonders of getting plastic surgery done in Tijuana, *gulp* **"Black and Blue Señorita."**

SLEEP NO MORE

Shake with Ice and strain into a chilled Collins glass:
1 oz. Vermouth
1¼ oz. Butterfly Pea Flower-Infused Vodka
½ oz. St. Germain Elderflower Liqueur
½ oz. Simple Syrup
To affect color-change from indigo–blue to lavender stir in:
¾ oz. fresh Lime Juice and top with 1 Splash of Dry Sparking Rosé.
Garnish with a Lavender Sprig.

I am 29 years old and I ask a stranger I met on an app to meet me IRL at the McKittrick Hotel in Chelsea on New Year's Eve because I want a re-do after that hotel room on Long Island.[27]

You tell him to meet you in the basement ballroom at 8pm. You'll be the one in the gold flapper dress and peacock headband bathed in blue light. A hand on your lower back alerts you; he's found you. You both take off the Bauta masks you received at the desk and smile. He's Bradley Cooper-level striking and fit in his tuxedo. Remasking your faces, he takes your hand and rushes you upstairs into the "Emursive" drama. Even though the bellhop warned you earlier that the hotel's theatrical atmosphere is "best experienced alone," you let the striking stranger whisk you through the residences on third floor, you giggle through the graveyard, skip back to the second floor, through the film-noir-lit lobby to find a pile of salt and a goat head and cutlery in the shape of crucifixes. He whispers in your ear that it's time for the fourth floor, the Village of Gallow Green. Running through a room with scattered hay on the floor, the tune "When the Swallows Come Back to Capistrano" plays strangely, and the stranger will pull you into a dark room near the Manderley Bar where he'll rip off your mask and kiss you with a primal hunger; against the wall he will kiss your neck and explore beneath your golden flapper dress until he's on his knees. When you're both done, you'll climb to the fifth floor, "the sanitorium" to find Lady MacBeth naked in a bathtub nearing the end of her second recursive loop. She stands, dripping wet. There's blood on her hands and she's screaming. She leaps at you before the nurses take her away.

Moments later, without a word to the stranger, you bolt down several flights back to New York City streets. And on the subway you notice the fake blood on your dress.

....
[27] *Pair with* **"Long Island"** and take a long, sad sip.

DANTICAT, EDWIDGE. *THE FARMING OF BONES.* PRINT.

You've spent all day taking intakes and filling out asylum applications for people from the Northern Triangle—Honduras, Guatemala, El Salvador. That's the most Spanish you've spoken (seven straight hours) in a long, long time. The two guys from Harvard Law don't speak it so they're sent home early—it's just you and the other Latina legal interns. You had no idea how to say "labor union" but you figured it out along the way ("sindicato"). Gangs, domestic violence, gangs, domestic violence all day. You get home that night and call your mom to tell her how you were giving legal help to immigrants in a federal building in lower Manhattan.

She's happy you're helping these people. She always told you how important it was for you to speak Spanish, she reminds you.[28] She hopes you'll become an immigration attorney and help others. She pauses. "And you can be a writer, too. All those stories people tell you; you can turn them into a book." You want to cry. She realizes something you've never really told her: you want to be *both*.

. . . .

[28] *See* **"William, Shakespeare"** or *sip* **"French Cosmopolitan."**

CANE AND COLA

2 oz. of discontinued 10-Cane Rum
(made from 1st press Trinidadian cane juice)
6 oz. MexiCoke
Mix in tall glass with Ice.
Garnish with wedge of Lime.

I am 7 years old and watching *Fresh Prince of Bel Air* and *Family Matters* and *Martin* when my dad comes home from work and asks me why I'm watching "esos negros" and to "get them off the screen." I tell him he shouldn't say it that way but give up on my speech halfway through and change the channel to Univisión for him.

You always thought your mom was a little more evolved about these sorts of things. And the summer between 1L and 2L, you try to explain to her that you were accepted on the law school's *Journal of Law & Race* and what that means. You also tell her that you watched a movie called *Loving* that made you cry because you're in an interracial relationship with The Editor, a man who lives in Virginia, and he is the first man you can really see yourself marrying, and within your mother's lifetime such a union had been illegal. The distance between California and New York feels even greater when she responds. *"But you're not Black,"* is all she can say.

DEFOE, DANIEL. *ROBINSON CRUSOE*. PRINT.

During a commercial break of *Montel*, my older brother Nacho gives me (his five-year-old sister) my first history lesson. I am sitting on the salmon-colored leather loveseat braiding my Day-to-Night Barbie's hair. My teenage sister is on the longer salmon-colored leather couch writing a love letter to some eighth-grade boy she has a crush on. Moments before, she and I were both emotionally invested in Montel's guests—who exactly was the father of the 18-year-old girl's baby? her stepfather? or the 14-year-old next door?—but now with the commercial we are tuned out to "what's coming up next on the 5 o'clock news."[29] Until my 19-year-old brother, who has been making a sandwich in the kitchen, marches up to the tv and beats once, then twice at his chest: "We were here first! We were here first, motherfuckers! This was Mexico," he roars. I look up to see people on the screen being interviewed at the San Diego border—all of them white-skinned with opinions about who does and doesn't belong.

Years later, I will learn *1848* was an important year and I will think of my brother beating at his chest, moments before Montel came back on the screen.

---

[29] For other instances of your teenage sister failing to monitor your television consumption, *see also* **"Carroll, Lewis."**

CREATIVE NATIVE

1½ oz. Rum (Bacardi)
1½ oz. Kahlua
1½ oz. Bailey's Irish Cream
1½ oz. Heavy Cream and Cracked Ice
Use blender to make a pale brown smoothie.
Serve in a frosty Hurricane glass.
Top with whipped cream as desired.

I am 6 years old and ask my daddy about all the Mexican men lined up on the blocks leading to Peachland Elementary School.

It's your daddy's day off and he is driving you to first grade in his khaki-colored pick-up on a Monday morning. On both sides of the street are men standing around, some laughing in groups, some leaning against fences with hungry eyes, ready to prove themselves.
"Why are those guys there, Daddy? It's cold outside."
"Necesitan chamba," your papi will say.
"Well how long will they have to wait until they get work?"
"Quizás todo el día," your papi will say. A few blocks later, your papi will drop you off in front of the school. You'll kiss your daddy goodbye on his cheek. Hanging your little pea coat and "Hakunah-Matata" backpack up in the classroom, you'll feel grateful your daddy doesn't have to wait outside in the cold in order to find a job, but will feel sorry for the men who look like him who do.

DÍAZ, JUNOT. *THIS IS HOW YOU LOSE HER.* PRINT.

Life with her was a blur. Sped up so she would never slow down to let the one-eyed Chinese father back in: the stains on her little, yellow, daisy-colored dress, hiding in the closet on days off from school, father-daughter time in the back of the Catholic bookstore, or watching porn in his lap when he should have been putting on *Looney Tunes*. She was your lover in a parallel universe; an instant best friend burning too hot in this one. You thought there was nothing she could ever do or say that would drive you away from her until there was. So, you pack. And that last month of living together you hear her snippets of Spanish to her mother, little conversations she has with the son she had at 16 who lives in New Mexico, and you hear each other make the flapper-era floor groan but don't say a word. A year later, you find one of her poems on a website—everywomanwehaveloved.com—and it's published in English and in Spanish. Addressed to a "Señorita," it reads, "your wine-stained teeth meet at the intersection of trainwreck and sexy." You put down your glass of cabernet next to your MacBook and can't shake the feeling you know who the señorita might be.

PINK PANTY PULLDOWNS

1 L. Sprite
2 cups Pink Lemonade
2 cups Vodka
Shake in an Ice-filled 2 gal. jug.
Dispense into mason jars.

I am 5 years old and I love my first Martha.

She combs my hair into a ponytail, pulls my pink-power-ranger panties up, pulls my dresses down over me, and ties the laces of my mountain boots. After I'm dressed, we watch *Dos Mujeres, Un Camino* before I go to kindergarten (I'm rooting for the brunette one). In the afternoons, she picks me up from the bus stop, scoops me into her arms, and, with the soft voice of a Mexican fairy princess, she whispers into my ear that she loves me. Most nights after my mom gets home from work, Martha's boyfriend visits her and I spy on them while they kiss hard in the front yard. This is the reason my mom tells me she has to let her go: "Martha cares more about her boyfriend than you."[30]

....

[30] Years and years later, over Monday night dinner with your family, your brother's second wife will drunkenly spill the beans, that the real reason Martha #1 was fired was because your brother Nacho was secretly fucking her and your mom found out.

DICK, PHILIP K. *DO ANDROIDS DREAM OF ELECTRIC SHEEP?* PRINT.

After watching a science-fiction movie we clearly did not understand, my blonde-haired childhood friend Kimberley and I go downstairs to my kitchen where my dad is making tacos for dinner.

Taco nights at Kimberley's house are usually on Tuesdays; tacos at my house are always five minutes away from being made. The ingredients are perennially in stock. At Kimberley's house, tacos are served promptly at the table at 7:30pm, the nightly news in the background. On the plate are usually two tacos made of soft Mission brand flour tortillas covered in Kraft shredded cheddar cheese accompanied by a large glass of Knudsen milk. A bottle of Heinz ketchup is passed around her family. At my house, my dad fills a corn tortilla with his seasoned meat and then deep-fries the tortilla in hot oil until it's hissing and crisp. He makes salsa from scratch—hot chili peppers burn on the comal. He cuts up aguacate from his friend's backyard for us to bite into.

Though my father and I usually stand at the kitchen counter to eat our tacos, we sit down at the table because Kimberley is a guest.[31] When my dad places a magnificent plate of tacos in front of Kimberley, salsa and all, she will look up at my dad with her big, beautiful, blue eyes and ask him politely for ketchup. When he looks back down at her, confused and pained, I tell him to sit and eat. I will get her ketchup for her.

. . . .

[31] For more on this white girl being a "guest," *sip* **"Island Toy."**

44

PUFF'S MAGICK DRAGON

Stir into large glass pitcher:
2 Packages Purple Grape Kool-Aid
2 cups Ice
1 Bottle Club Soda
½ Bottle Hot Damn! (cinnamon schnaps)
Dispense into paper Dixie Cups.

I am 25 years old and I am convinced that I am going to float away, I am so stoned. *That's why they call it getting high,* I think as my bland epiphany and high hit their crescendo.

Though I drank with the best of them, I always refused to smoke marijuana in high school, so my first experience actually comes in graduate school at a house by the sea. Heading to the beach in Georgia for spring break with a few friends, we spend most of our days rocking on the porch, eating shrimp and grits, and finding shells along the beach. My red-haired freckle-faced pseudo lover from my program is there and, in the mornings, we sit on the porch together and laugh while everyone is still asleep. It's the kind of flirtatious laughter everyone can pick up on, including her husband. When I get stoned for the first time, I ask her to hold my hands, "or else I'll float away," I say. She does, and I thank her for keeping me on this earth. Our hands crisscrossed and locked, we look intensely into each other's eyes for what feels like hours. Tears start to form and then we laugh endlessly.

In the backseat on the ride back to Washington, DC, when her husband falls asleep, she will put her hands on my lap and say, "He's asleep." She'll lean in further: "Now we can play." The magic of the week coming to an end, I will look at her lovingly but then roll my eyes and return to staring at the scenery of interstate.[32]

. . . .

[32] For more on the red-haired girl, *see also* **"Twain, Mark"** or *sip* **"Silk Panties with Lace"** and take another *gulp of* **"Freight Train."** And for more on lovers that make your eyes roll, *sip* **"Adios Motherfucker."**

DICKENS, CHARLES. A TALE OF TWO CITIES. PRINT.

"Yo voy a regresar a mi home," your dad always says. Whenever you tell him something mildly accusatory or when your mom tells him she doesn't like the shirt he's wearing or she needs help paying bills for the house, he'll threaten to move back to Mexico, "Voy a vivir en MI casa y ustedes me pueden visitar y pueden chupar sus mangos si no quieren venir."

He came to the United States when he was 16, worked for a year packing meat in snowy Omaha, and saved money to buy his parent's a home in Mexico. He later settled in Los Angeles in the late 1960s. Still, he pines for his México lindo. He pines for that rancho querido near Tenamaxtlán where he grew up in a one-room shack with nine brothers and sisters eating beans for three meals a day and riding horses into the mountains with his father.

When your dad is in his early 60s, you'll ask him, half in English and half in Spanish: "You've lived in this country por mucho más tiempo que viviste en México, isn't this your home?

BORDER CROSSING

Pour in a short glass with Ice:
1½ oz. Tequila
2 tsp. Lime Juice
1 tsp. Lemon Juice
Top up with:
4 oz. Mexicoke
Garnish lip with 4 Lime Wheels.

I am 12 years old, exit my family's red Lincoln Navigator, and set my clean converse sneakers down on the dusty cobblestones in Mexico.

I walk to the stand on the side of the road with my dad and he buys me a cup of half pineapple/half papaya from the girl with the dark-brown skin who is my height. Flies surround the girl but all the fruit she sells is tightly covered. I feel her hungry eyes follow me as I make my way back to the passenger seat.

When my dad pulls away, an army of young Mexican boys will climb on the car and swarm the windshield, begging for pesos. "Quítense cabrones," my dad will yell. Still, he'll toss pesos out of the window, and I'll see tiny brown hands in the rearview mirror picking the coins off the ground.

DOSTOEVSKY, FYODOR. *CRIME AND PUNISHMENT.* PRINT.

I thought he was my cousin for so long. I had seen him come almost every year to my house on Thanksgiving and he never noticed me until the year I wore that orange polka dot dress that made his eyes hungry. Months later he came into my dorm room and unzipped his pants only minutes after he entered, and then zipped them right up and left only moments after it happened. My roommate called campus police and they eventually came to collect my sheets and the metallic magenta dress I had been wearing. The following week my mother arranged a meeting with his mother. We met at my mom's work, at her beauty salon in North Hollywood. My sister held my hand as I sat in the manicurist's chair, and I read from the two-page single-spaced sequence of events I had typed the night before. It was hard to look at his mother after but I'm glad I told his mami on him because I've never had to see his deceiving face in my house again.[33]

. . . .

[33] *Pair also with* **"The Blood of Satan."**

SUNDAY CONFESSION

1 oz. White Tequila
1 oz. Limoncello
½ oz. Lemon Juice
Top up with 2 oz. Ginger Beer
Garnish with a single Dark Cherry.

I am 19 years old and I tell my mom and my sister how it started.

He hasn't stopped texting me since he saw me last Thanksgiving dinner. It progressed. I felt lonely, I gave in, and I invited him to my dorm room, but I didn't mean for it to end the way it did. It felt like he was punishing me for my scattered attention all those months. My mother confesses an uncle molested her when she was 9 years old. It started with a glass of milk. My sister confesses a cousin from México who lived with us one summer molested her in the early 90s. It started with a back massage. I confess I swallowed my distant cousin's cum that I didn't want to swallow. It started with a text message. We all agree we can't tell my father.

ELIOT, GEORGE. *MIDDLEMARCH.* PRINT.

Whenever you are having problems with men, your papi will offer to arrange a marriage for you.[34c] "If your life were a Mexican sitcom I could find you a cowboy in Mexico," would almost certainly be your daddy's catchphrase—if he had one. Can't find a date for prom? "Te puedo conseguir un charro en México." Having problems with a boyfriend? "Te puedo conseguir un charro." Need someone to open a jar of tomato sauce? "Te puedo conseguir un cowboy muy cowboy."

You always laugh and then give him a hug and kiss for offering. Sometimes you indulge him: "would the cowboy have green eyes," you ask?

"Light skin, blue eyes—whatever you want—lo que tú quieras," he'll say. In the end, you always tell him that you'll figure it out on your own. He will go back to circling horse racing statistics from his newspaper, the only numbers he seems to understand, chuckle to himself in English that "the ladies are too complicated," and when you start to walk away, he will remind you that the offer is always on the table.

. . . .

[34] *See also*…well *see* everything, really.

POOKY AND CHOOKY

2 oz. Milk
2 oz. Irish Cream
2 oz Pisang Ambon (bright green banana liqueur)
1 oz. Vodka (Smirnoff)
Shake with Ice until pale green.
Strain into 2 cocktail glasses.

I am 16 years old and hear snippets of stories about my abuelita and abuelito—my father's parents.

There are the basics, of course: They were from a very small pueblo in Jalisco called Juanacatlán, they had nine children, and lived in a one-room shack.

My abuelita doesn't enjoy being photographed, and any rare attempt to capture her ends up in a shot where her arms are crossed, giving the camera a dirty pissed-off stare.

My abuelito wakes up at dawn and everywhere he goes he wears his poncho, which swishes through the door as if he were a Mexican Batman. When my abuelito was a young man he drank often, rode his horses, and shot his guns, much to my abuelita's anguish.

In their old age they settle into a large house my father purchases for them in Tenamaxtlán with his American wages. Even with all their children and grandchildren they live among a lot of empty rooms that only really get filled in December during the fiestas. When he returns from the market or some other errand, my abuelito whistles loudly in the cavernous casa to let my abuelita know he is home. My abuelito will die first, even though my abuelita had been the sickly one, in bed for so long. A few months after that, two of my tías will be feeding my abuelita on her deathbed. They will ask her why she keeps smiling. My abuelita will tell them it is because a handsome man in the corridor won't stop whistling at her.

ELLISON, RALPH. *INVISIBLE MAN.* PRINT.

The first young man I feel strong enough to date after my father passes away[35] is a half-Black, half-Jewish gentleman who lives in Harlem. He is five years younger than me and that is a first.[36] Our first date is tacos in Nolita. In a bar not too far from that, with Mexican men cheering in the background watching a soccer match, I tell him about my dad; he tells me about his mom. A woman who was once a doctor at NYU but had an aneurysm, so she isn't quite the mother he knew anymore. After another round of Pisco Sours, we kiss on the bar stools, as if no one in the crowded bar could see us. Magical dates in the city follow. Walking the length of Central Park hand in hand in the July rain, kissing somewhere on the east side near the museums. Feeding each other deep-fried barbecue squid on St. Marks. Catching one of the last performances of *Angels in America* with Nathan Lane after I win cheap tickets in the Broadway lottery. Making aggressive love in his bedroom during a summer storm—the thunder masking the screams I make when he bites down hard across my back, arms, neck and digs his fingers into my hips—so his brother in the next room won't hear us. All the bites will bloom into a fleshy moss-mustard field of bruises I hide under tailored blazers at the law office. The bruises will fade during the workweek until it's time to see him again and he can apply fresh ones.

. . . .

[35] *See also* "Cather, Willa."

[36] For the reason why, *see* "Bukowski, Charles."

¡HALLELUJAH IUD!

1½ oz. Gin (Citadell)
1 oz Dolin Blanc
1 oz. Aveze
1 dash Peychaud's
Layer ingredients over an expressed Lemon Peel.

I am 28 years old and the 23-year-old I am seeing fingers me relentlessly under a vintage cardigan I have positioned over my legs in Tompkins Square Park.

We are surrounded by at least one hundred *Film on the Green* moviegoers. Luckily, my gasps and shortness of breath are appropriate considering we are watching a 1970s French thriller about a butcher. As he pushes a digit past my overly peppered mound, I find that his afro is the most divine cushion for my cheek to rest on.[37] Naturally, this little foreplay in the park leads to hungry, relentless fucking uptown. So relentless neither of us will notice when the condom slips off and gets sucked into my vagina. Because he is a gentleman, he will reach in and grab it for me. The next day, I consult message boards. How common is it to lose a condom inside of you? Why does no one tell you about this? Does a rogue rubber run the risk of dislodging an IUD? Why does being a woman come with more questions than answers? Fed up with the Internet, I take myself to urgent care and start blushing in front of the doctor when I recount the story. She starts probing. "I think I can see the strings," she says. But my sigh of relief is short lived when she tells me it is actually just a coarse black hair and holds it up to the light for me to see.[38]

. . . .

[37] You can't afford Brazilian waxes at this time, after all.

[38] For more on IUD concerns and contraception generally, *gulp down* **"Creamy Punani."**

ESQUIVEL, LAURA. *COMO AGUA PARA CHOCOLATE / LIKE WATER FOR CHOCOLATE*. PRINT.

The cake of magical realism that made everyone cry . . . and you also took a big ol' bite. You first heard about this book on a cobble-stoned car ride in a dusty pueblo in México. Your older cousin Erica was reading it and it sparked your interest, especially given the "horse scene" everyone was whispering about in the car, the scene that they said you were too young to know about. Like Tita, you were the youngest daughter in your Mexican family but unlike Tita you wouldn't be expected to forego marriage and watch your older sister marry the man of your dreams. Thank goodness they axed that wonderful tradition of the youngest daughter taking care of her parents until they die. You see, you were born in America, and your parents will have Medicare and Social Security to aid them in their old age (though *you* might not, given the way the media reports it and the rich bastards want to slice it). Every chapter begins with a new recipe and the "quail in rose petal sauce" washes over you still. The ending, the title, is how you try to live your life: passionate and breathless at a boil.

MEXICAN BURNING VILLAGE

½ oz. Tequila
½ oz. Bacardi 151 Proof Rum
Pepper Flakes
Dash(es) Hot Sauce
Cover the bottom of a shot glass with Pepper Flakes.
Add rum, add tequila, add dashes of hot sauce.
Seal your hand over the mouth of the glass so it won't spill.
Flip. Watch the flakes swirl down (like a snow globe)
like flaming embers. Put it right side up again
. . . lick your palm . . . and Shoot!

I am 17 years old and tell my mother about the time I was 5 years old and I saw my daddy dancing in the town square in Mexico with the doctor's wife. Real close.

My mother had already flown back to Los Angeles to work at the beauty salon, and we would be leaving in the Mazda minivan the next day. His sisters stood in judgment. Too much tequila they said. Fresh from church, my abuelita ripped off her black veil and brought my father home by his ear. She let me wear his Stetson all the way home. It's been years since this happened, so I thought my mother knew the story. When my father came home from dios knows where, she yelled at him with a grito that pierced the length of the suburban block.

EUGENIDES, JEFFREY. *MIDDLESEX*. PRINT.

One of two authors that made you go mad with envidia with their first lines alone.[39] You've been wild about Greece and Greek mythology for years and all roads seem to have led you to this novel, when you first find it in high school.[40]

But by the time you meet Eugenides at Skylight Books in Los Feliz, years later, he's signing copies of *The Marriage Plot* that afternoon, and you go drink at the tavern across the street, alone, beforehand. You arrive drunk after imbibing at least five cocktails (you lost count, after all) and say lord knows what to Jeffrey. He signs your copy, but he looks worried for your wellbeing.

. . . .

[39] *See* **"Morrison, Toni"** (and everything she ever wrote) for untarnished novels that have stood the test of time.

[40] While this may have been one of your favorites in high school, when a professor later tells you that the book is very problematic on 1,000,000 levels, "number 1 being its cis, white, male author's willingness to benefit (Pulitzer-prize-winning benefit, no less!) from the appropriation and exoticization of queer, trans, intersex, and women's under-represented literary voices, as well as our erased life experiences . . ." Eugenides's *Middlesex* will start to lose a bit of its luster.

TRIPLESEX

In a Hurricane glass, add:
2 parts Smirnoff Vodka
2 parts Triple Sec
3 parts Sweet and Sour
Pineapple Juice to taste
Garnish with a slice of Tangerine thrown on the grill
for an extra layer of smokey complexity.

I am 19, 20, 21, 22, 23, 24, 25, 26, 27, 28 and I receive a lot of threesome propositions.

When the men I am dating and/or sleeping with find out that I am a bisexual Latina, I can see the threesome-cha-ching in their eyes. The first one to suggest a threesome must have been the comedian/screenwriter/ production designer's friend, who was a screenwriter in his own right. He told me he knew "a nice MILF in Sherman Oaks who might be interested," but while it's an idea that gets me hot for a hot minute, it only sounds great—in *theory*. I'm unsure how it would play out in *practice* given my overall brand of indie awkwardness. So, I never seriously considered it until I met that married woman in my graduate program. The one with the red hair like my childhood friend's. She and her husband will escort me to the bus stop near their apartment in Columbia Heights after a night of bar hopping, "I'm wearing him down," she'll whisper into my ear.[41]

....

[41] For more on this red-haired señorita, *also sip* **"Silk Panties with Lace."**

FAULKNER, WILLIAM. *THE SOUND AND THE FURY.* PRINT.

My older brother Nacho, a former soldier, found me crying in my room after my mom told me I couldn't wear overalls to the wedding we were going to that day. She said I had to wear a dress. My brother thumbed through all my pretty dresses in my closet and told me I was lucky. When he was a little boy in the 70's all my parents could afford were second-hand clothes. He distinctly remembers my mother buying him a pair of "girl's" jeans with a Wonder Woman patch on the rear. My mom didn't understand who Wonder Woman was, so she didn't understand that they were girl's jeans. I was lucky because my parents moved to a better area, and I was in a good school. When he was a little boy, he was placed in ESL classes because all he ever spoke was Spanish at home. I was lucky because I wouldn't have to enlist like he did, I wouldn't have to go fight in Somalia like he did. Years later when my father kicked me out of the house for a month, I called my brother in tears and he told me that I shouldn't expect anything from anyone, not even our parents.[42] "No battle is ever won," he said.

---

[42] *Pair with* "**Black and Blue Señorita.**"

SCREAMING PORNSTAR

In a tulip glass with Ice, add:
2 oz. Vodka (Vanilla flavored)
½ oz. Passoa (passionfruit liqueur)
1½ fresh Passionfruits
½ oz. lime juice, fresh squeezed
Sprinkle Rose Petals on top.

I am 9 years old and my mom is making sopes and tortas for dinner on Monday night, her regular day off from work.

My mother invites my 23-year-old brother to the house and serves him a full plate of food and calls him her rey. He's moved into an apartment in the San Fernando Valley and the car-selling business is going well. He starts telling my father that he's been dating an actress. His eyes are expressive and he says he's started dating one of those actresses. He smirks. My mom and my sister are confused. I spit out my frijoles and tell the table I really don't want to hear about his "exploits" while I'm eating my favorite foods. Everyone laughs. No one expected the child to understand.[43]

....

[43] For more on porn and pornstars, *see* **"Plath, Sylvia."**

FITZGERALD, F. SCOTT. *TENDER IS THE NIGHT.* PRINT.

You lose your virginity the night before you jet off to Europe. You'll be studying abroad in London for a semester. It'll be your junior year of college. You've worked a summer job at a high-end movie theater in the San Fernando Valley where you met the comedian/screenwriter/production designer. He'll have just moved into a new apartment in Reseda and won't have any furniture. He'll fuck you on the floor and your back will be rammed into a wall for a good 10 minutes.[44] It'll feel tender for a few days. You'll find poetry in the fact that you hopped aboard Virgin Airlines, no longer a virgin on your first ever transatlantic voyage. You won't mess around with anyone in Europe because you'll be waiting to come back to him and when you do, he won't want you anymore. He'll say you're clingy and he's not ready for a relationship. When he is ready a few months later, he casts some other long-haired Latina in the role of his girlfriend. It'll crush you how much she looks like you.[45]

....

[44] If that. You didn't see a clock that night so 10 minutes might be an incredibly generous estimation.

[45] For other instances of men picking the other long-haired Latina, *see* **"Huxley, Aldous."**

SILK PANTIES WITH LACE

For this shooter, gather:
1 oz. Vodka
½ oz. Peach Schnapps
1 Lemon
Dash(es) Sugar
Rim the shot glass and coat a Lemon Wedge with Sugar.
Bite down on the Lemon before you take the shot.

I am 24 years old and packing up to move out of my parents' house for a graduate school program across the country.

I find my favorite pair of underwear in my mother's laundry basket. It's been months since I've seen this pair and I worry my mom has been wearing my favorite lace panties to bed with my father. There's no use confronting her about it. I still have a similar pair. I'll be wearing those panties on a night in my new city when I will feel the diamond on a wedding ring scratch my inner thigh underneath the table. The wedding ring belongs to a girl in my program. It will sting a little, but I won't let her husband, who is sitting across from me, suspect.

FLAUBERT, GUSTAVE. *MADAME BOVARY.* PRINT.

You start sleeping with a Harvard Law professor of Mexican descent (with sons about your age) during 2L. The Harvard Law professor visits New York City periodically and he meets you at Grand Central Station when he does.[46] In certain lights he reminds you of Diego Rivera and you later find out that he has a wife, much like Diego did. Her name is Rosa, like your mother, and his wife is a Virgo, just like you. The first time you meet will be at Dos Caminos, after he gives you the choice between sushi and "bad Mexican." "Was that some kind of double entendre?" you'll ask during pillow talk.

In the months that follow, you and he tend to share paella mixta and pitchers of sangria de vino tinto at a Spanish restaurant around the corner from the station called La Fonda del Sol. He has a hypothesis about why you tend to pick that restaurant. "You're too ashamed to walk with me in the city," he will tease. Unsure if that is true, you continue sipping your sangria with a lady-like air, brushing your foot against his under the table, and discussing the finer points of equal protection legislation. He will take a call during the meal. It will be his girlfriend, Sandra, in Texas. "It's important—she needs me right now…okay?" You make a quick joke about feeling like a woman in a Fellini film. But ultimately, you'll nod, then finish off the pitcher before he returns.

. . . .

[46] For more on your attraction to older men, *see also* **"Bukowski, Charles."**

SUICIDE STOP LIGHT

Line up three shot glasses and pour into:
#1. 1½ parts Midori Green Melon Liqueur
#2. 1½ parts Absolut Vodka
#3. 1½ oz. (red) Aftershock
Splash Orange Juice into #2 with the Vodka for yellow color
Shoot: green, yellow, red.

I am 14 years old and think about how I would do it.

Alone on a Saturday night, you consider pills. But the thought of your parents finding you that way on the couch after coming back that night from their *parientes'* wedding in Bakersfield pulls you back. You write an essay for 9th grade English class about having those thoughts, and almost going about it. You'll get an "A-"-on the essay, your English teacher commenting that from a craft standpoint, the source of your depression is unclear. That takes up a few sentences. The rest of the page is devoted to reminding you how wonderful he thinks you are and how sorry he is to know you felt that way. He will refer you to your high school counselor. You fool her into thinking you're okay—your perfect grades help with that—and then beg her not to tell your parents. These thoughts come back your last year of high school and your first year of law school. Watching the snow collect in the courtyard outside your Manhattan apartment and your loans stacking up in your inbox, you'll think how comfortable that snow looks from twelve stories high.[47] But, after hearing your mom tell you she wanted to commit suicide after the first month of your father's passing,[48] your suicidal ideations will come to an end. For good. "Please don't give up, Mommy," you'll tell her. "We need you more than ever."

. . . .

[47] *See also* "**Kafka, Franz.**"

[48] *See also* "**Cather, Willa.**"

FORSTER, E.M. *HOWARDS END.* PRINT.

With a mother who spent hours on her feet every day at her beauty salon,[49] so much so that I rarely saw her at home during my childhood, I wish she didn't feel as if she worked her whole life with nothing to show for it. It's not like my mom isn't a success—a Mexican family living in the white suburbs was no simple feat. She sacrificed everything for us to live in that cookie-cutter home, paid all the bills largely by herself. I remind her of this, but in her endless loop she tells me of all the properties my dad told her to sell in the late 1980s so that he could keep up racetracks across Southern California (though she didn't know it then). "They would be worth so much now," she says. "We could have had so much more," she tells me. Though she doesn't name them, I know she must also think of her hermanitos, the ones who were also born with nothing in Mexico. Her younger brothers in America, each with their own successful businesses. Each one with real estate properties of their own. One with a successful restaurant he later sells for more than half a million, so a Starbucks can be built in its place.

....

[49] For more on the beauty salon, *see* **"Marx, Karl"** and for more on your hardworking mother, *sip* **"American Beauty."**

MEXICAN STAND-OFF

In a 5-Gallon Vitrolero, "Made in Mexico," plastic container
(half-filled with Ice)
Mix:
350 cl. Vodka
350 cl. White Tequila (Jose Cuevo)
350 cl. Passoa
Ladle into hand-painted clay jugs

I am 7 years old and I am one of only two little Mexican girls
in Mrs. Nishioka's 2nd grade class

All the other Mexican girls and boys—at least thirty of them—are across
the quad in Mrs. Herman's class. As I line up after recess, I wonder why
I'm not in a class with little kids who look like me. Because when we
stare at each other from across the way, their big brown eyes meet mine
and question why I'm in a class with mostly blue-eyed white kids.

The big projects Mrs. Nishioka's class does every year: mold the Statute
of Liberty out of clay and make *Cloudy with a Chance of Meatballs*
meatballs; Mrs. Herman's class always learns how to sing las mañanitas
and make buñuelos. My Lady Liberty won't be perfect, but the gray clay
of her robe will hide the green-white-red snake-eating eagle I also am,
the one biting at her legs beneath.[50]

----

[50] For more on the battle to retain your Mexican heritage, *see also* **"O'Brien, Tim"**
and **"Shakespeare, William"** *or sip* **"French Cosmopolitan."**

GOLDING, WILLIAM. *LORD OF THE FLIES.* PRINT.

Blue-eyed Kimberley holds the conch and casts you out to sea. For so much of high school you drank alcohol on Fridays and Saturdays with those white girls and boys[51] but your parents never suspected because your grades were still perfect and they thought you really were sleeping over at Kimberley's or Laura's.[52] But the lies spun out of control the moment the car is suspended in mid-air and you become hysterical when the car lands back on its wheels and when you see the boy who had been sitting in the passenger seat with blood dripping down his hair from all the broken glass. This blonde All-American cheerleader has been your "best friend" since you were five but when her boy toy, who once dabbled in Neo-Nazism, says he's "done with your brown ass because you overreacted when the car flipped three times,"[53] she's done with your brown ass and they're *all* done with your brown ass.[54]

· ·

[51] *See also* "**Wharton, Edith.**"

[52] For more on the white girls down the street, *see also* "**Dick, Philip K.**" or *sip* "**Island Toy.**"

[53] *See also* "**Shelley, Mary.**"

[54] But you know now it's for the best. Because when the cholas in high school talked shit to her, she always defended herself by saying that her *best friend* was Mexican and told everyone she was so special because she was an eighth Cherokee.

COLD WAR

Ice and shake: 1½ oz. Jagermeister
1 oz. Vodka
12 oz. Red Bull Energy Drink
Sour Mix
Strain into an Old-fashion glass
over a formidable chunk of Block Ice.

I am 26 years old and experiencing my second break-up that year.

In June I had said so-long to my long-distance boyfriend. And in July I met The Editor, became his girlfriend in August, and was dumped by September. The Editor and I only dated for two months but the relationship was like a poem: so much meaning and love condensed in such brief space. Not only that but I had real telenovela-level fights with boyfriends in the past that weren't deal breakers and our fight was nothing like that.[55] When he does it, he's crying, too, and his eyes are bluer than I've ever seen. After, I delete and block him on *Facebook* and *Google chat*. I break down in tears every day in the shower. I ignore a text he sends me in October asking if I want a dress I left at his condo. I pass out on my apartment stairs with no pants and a bottle of wine next to me and my roommate's lover finds me there when he goes out for a smoke. The Editor finds me again on New Year's Day of the following year and I tell him all this. He nods and shares that when his wife left him for her high school sweetheart, he'd drink whiskey by himself many mornings before working his shift at *The Washington Post*.

. . . .

[55] *Sip* **"Lord and Lady."**

HANSBERRY, LORRAINE. *A RAISIN IN THE SUN.* PRINT.

In the photos of your father's 70th birthday celebration, you notice your 60-something mother looks absolutely glowing. Your father, brother, sister, and you all clean up quite nicely, but there is just something in your mom's cheeks that almost sparkles and you cannot quite put your finger on it.

A few months after the celebration you get your answer when your mother willingly confesses over the phone: "your papi got me botox." You know you shouldn't be surprised given your parent's history with plastic surgery in Tijuana and all the perfectly lacquered telenovela faces you grew up watching in your house.[56] And by this point in your life, you *aren't* surprised. You only push back a little when your mom launches into the defensive before you even take a breath. "It's just that your papi doesn't want me looking like a raisin. He wants me to look beautiful. He always wants me to look my best and not like an old lady," she says.

"Mami, you will always be beautiful to me," you say, "with or without the botox."

---

[56] *Also sip* **"Black and Blue Señorita"** and for more on the things your mother does to her face, *see also* **"Thackeray, William Makepeace."**

CAMPESINA

In an Old-Fashioned glass with Crushed Ice, add:
2 ½ oz. Tequila
2 tsp. Sugar
1 Lime, cut into 8 wedges
served with 2 small straws.

I am 27 years old and my law school resume is in desperate need of a touch-up.

You consult the examples given to you by student services. Most of them have generic sounding "white" names like "Sam Smith" or "Sarah Williams" as if those are the only names that go to law school. On one sample, you notice "Sam Smith" received a full scholarship to undergraduate, not unlike yourself. In fact, you received full tuition scholarships to both undergraduate and graduate school. On your current resume, you have it listed as "full tuition scholarship," believing that alone is impressive. However, "Sam Smith" has opted to describe it as a *"merit-based* full tuition scholarship" (emphasis added). Your scholarships were merit-based, too. But you realize now that the phrasing you used, coupled with the "Zapata" surname, probably made you look to most as if you were a poor peasant the schools felt sorry for. Prospective employers might concede you were smart but might attribute your gains more to being Mexican as the sole reason and not just one factor.

You make the necessary changes to play their game, even though each letter you type hurts—because you know Sam Smith didn't have to deal with this.[57]

---

[57] For more on white people and scholarships, *see also* **"Twain, Mark"** or *sip* **"James the Second Comes First."**

HARDY, THOMAS. *TESS OF THE D'URBERVILLES.* PRINT.

The week before my first year of law school begins in New York City, my boyfriend The Editor treats me to a road trip across Virginia, with an emphasis on the countryside and backwoods. Jason Isbell love songs play as our soundtrack. We start the trip eating a dish called a "stuffin' muffin" and also "angels on the half shell" at a table on the edge of the Rappahannock. Sitting in the new vintage dress I bought especially for the occasion, my boyfriend tells me how pretty and feminine I always look. We then travel through the most majestic part of U.S. Route 1—green leafy canopies hang like blankets above us across the entire stretch to Star Hill Brewery. We get lost in a vineyard where rescue doggies sit in the sun and protect the grapes from the Chesapeake's voracious wildlife. Sometimes red barns, *real* red barns, sprout from the lushness. It is all so mesmerizing I cannot help but state the obvious: it is *so green.* The last part of the trip is a cabin in the woods of the Shenandoah Valley. But it's also the 2016 Olympics so my boyfriend fiddles with the television in the corner until he's streaming. Meanwhile, his border collie and I retreat to the back porch. I read essays by *Wise Latinas* in the rocking chair, sipping whiskey and listening to the soft hum of insects all around. I tell him I am taking the *Wise Latinas* to the bedroom. "Sounds crowded," he says. In the morning, birds singing in the trees, I try to mount my blue-eyed boyfriend to make love to him but he says he's too tired from all the driving. He's been tired for days. I take matters into my own hands, as I usually do, while he is on the other side of the bed, scrolling through his twitter and reading all the news headlines from the morning. My body comes with a loud sigh.[58]

. . . .

[58] For more on sharing a bed with The Editor, *see also* **"Kundera, Milan."**

SIT ON MY FACE, MARY JANE

In a shot glass, gather:
1 part Bailey's Irish Cream
1 part Frangelico
1 part Crown Royal
Shake until mixed together
and top with Whipped Cream.

I am 29 years old, it is my third year of law school, and I am hooking up with a 2L who lives across the city street.

While law school is still no picnic,[59] at least I am able to read cases on a crowded subway now; during 1L, I could only read case law in pin-drop silence, and even then it read like hieroglyphics. It's the first week of classes when he messages me, asking if I want "an afternoon *snack*." He comes to my apartment and we move to my bedroom.
"I haven't had an afternoon delight in a very long time," I tell him.
"I should be in class," he says.
"I should be in the library," I say.
He sits on my bed and gives me the best cold-call question: "Do you want to sit on my face?"
"Now that's a question I can answer," I say.
We certainly are not in love—far, far from it—but with him I hear sounds escape me that I didn't even know were possible. He is of African descent and his middle name is something beautiful I cannot pronounce.
"Does that name mean something?" I ask him.
"God sent you," he says.
"Yes, yes he did," I say.
Near the end, he asks his question again.
My body gives him another affirmative answer and I sit, grateful he's choosing my vagina on that rainy Tuesday afternoon over his Corporations class.

. . . .

[59] *See also* **"Kafka, Franz."**

HAWTHORNE, NATHANIEL. *THE SCARLET LETTER*. PRINT.

You're no Puritan like Hester Prynne, but you were raised in a Roman Catholic household and there are certain things you don't do in a Roman Catholic household. Have sex out of wedlock, for example. That's why you're one for taking it in the backseat of your car instead, so hard that a friend of the comedian/screenwriter/production designer makes you bleed. The morning after, your father borrows your car and asks you about a bit of blood he cleaned up in the backseat. He wonders if you're okay. You tell him it was a bloody nose and silently ask God for forgiveness.[60]

....

[60] For other bloody tales that go down less than smooth, *pair also with* **"Miscarriage."**

THE LEG SPREADER

Fill a cocktail shaker with:
1 oz. 1800 Tequila
1 oz. Vodka
1 oz. Gin
1 oz. Rum
And strain into a shot glass until you shudder.

I am 21 years old and I am making the most of the fact that my 21st birthday has fallen on a Monday at the beginning of the school year.

My roommates throw me a party despite the fact that we all have Tuesday classes. I come home to a "Corona" cake—over 40 Corona bottles stacked on a four-level tiered platform. All my guests bring me bottles of liquor, mostly Jack Daniels and Jameson, because they know me so well. Someone invites a South African guy who's in town visiting. I give him blue balls and he gives me the best present I could have asked for—a taste of cunnilingus. My first, in fact. I forgot his name, but I'll never forget how well he traversed Cape Town.

HELLER, JOSEPH. *CATCH-22*. PRINT.

When you were in fourth grade, your mom and dad's decision to start leasing new Lincoln Navigators every year didn't seem like a sound investment. Once, even as a little girl, you told them it probably wasn't practical, but they didn't listen. And you were torn too, because there was something about the smell of the leather seats and riding high in the suburban neighborhood in the red one, the white one, the silver one, the beige one. There was something about riding in the passenger seat next to your mom with your white childhood friends buckled in the back. There was something about sipping coffee or cocoa out of the complimentary mugs the dealership had given your family. There was something about driving on dusty cobblestoned streets on trips to Mexico in something so nice.

AMBUSH

*Pour:
1 oz. Amaretto
1 oz. Bushmill's Irish Whiskey
Into a mug of Hot Coffee.*

I am 26 years old and I am in an English graduate program with several conservative female Republicans.

Girls from places in Ohio, Georgia, Arkansas, and even the more insulated offerings of California. Though I gravitated toward all the liberal-minded ladies and gentlemen in my cohort, we all still had to share the communal graduate lounge for our printing and studying needs. Nestled on a hilltop overlooking the Potomac, it's the kind of campus where Joe Biden, Bernie Sanders, and even Hillary Clinton are invited to speak. After returning from Bernie's talk on the economy, the subject of Bush comes up in the graduate lounge. All the conservative girls sigh and say how much they miss the Bush years and how much they and their families idolize Newt Gingrich and John McCain. I am printing out the works of Luce Irigaray and Monique Wittig when my comrade in the program shouts across the room in disbelief: "But we study literature—I thought we were all communists?!"

HEMINGWAY, ERNEST. *THE SUN ALSO RISES.* PRINT.

I ask him to meet me at the Lincoln Memorial. On the phone, he tells me I'm the girl he wants to marry. He tells me I'm a fine girl. He just can't see me right now. He misses my almond eyes, but he can't see them. He tells me he's doing the Mexican thing. He's doing what Mexican men do when the woman they love destroys them. He's drunk. Quite drunk. He tells you he feels like the Mexican Jake Barnes. He's in the same city as the woman he loves, but he can't be with her. Not really. I explain that he's not impotent and I'm not romancing Spanish bullfighters so it's not exactly the same. In the end, despite my pleading, the Mexican Jake Barnes flies back to Los Angeles without meeting me and he tells this Señorita that if she ever comes back to Los Angeles, to call him and they can grab an Horchata Latte together at Tierra Mia and talk about what could have been.[61]

....

[61] *Pair also with* **"Adios Motherfucker."**

SUFFERING BASTARD, A SLIGHT VARIATION

In a Tiki Mug over Ice, add:
1 oz. Gin
1 oz. Rum
1 oz. Ginger Ale
½ oz. Lime Juice
With dash(es) of Bitters

He is 27 years old and he has four days left in a city that isn't his. He misses Los Angeles. His elderly Mexican mother needs him. He took a week off work and for what? He's crunched the numbers: It's cheaper to go stay in Maryland for the rest of the week renting a room in the home of a complete stranger rather than purchase a ticket back.

He wanders around the DMV drunk and refuses to see the girl he came for.[62]

---

[62] Warning: This one goes down much harder than **"Absolut La La Land"** but when he gives you chlamydia (*sip* **"Feel The Burn"**), you won't feel so bad for him anymore.

HOMER. *THE ODYSSEY.* PRINT.

You meet The Handsome Italian in front of a statute of Athena at The Met. He removes and checks your coat that protected you from the February snow. He is the kind of man worth sifting and swiping for, through the river of shit on Tinder.[63] You knew it when you saw his "About Me" was in Latin: *video meliora proboque deteriora sequor.* And it was confirmed when he told you, as you walked up the marble steps, that his favorite book was Homer's ancient epic. He is well versed in ancient Greek and Latin—languages he studied at the Harvard of Italy. He had asked you to send him some of your poetry beforehand. You did and he tells you his favorites, how beautiful he thought they were and how beautiful he thinks you are. You try to focus on the jade and gold pieces from Central America and Mexico you came to see together from the *Golden Kingdoms* exhibit, what the New Yorker called "jaw-dropping." But his jaw is dropping at the sight of you and his eyes won't stop following you as you move through the galleries. He tells you this, even. And you feel it, but almost can't believe it. He is so handsome that fiesta bells are indeed chiming in your chest.

In the sweetest of Italian accents, he asks you (as you're leaving The Met), "Where do you love . . ." (you both chuckle) ". . . I mean 'live'? . . . But I think we both know I have *love* on the brain."

. . . .

[63] *See also* **"McCullers, Carson"** or *sip* **"Red Alert."**

GREEK SEX ON THE BEACH

In a Collins glass, add:
2 parts Vodka
1½ parts Bacardi Limon
2 parts Grenadine
2½ parts Orange Juice
Garnish with Greek Orange slices.

I am 28 years old and I ask the naked Italian man sprawled out next to
me to whisper some ancient Greek into my ear.

Later that morning, he will open the blinds to reveal the snow falling on
the Upper East Side. It is the first day of my spring break from law school.
Aside from the snow, I could imagine I was in Greece—the white crisp
linens of the bed and the blue calmness of the walls undulate warmly
within my brain. I'll think back to our first date the month before—how
I asked him to wear a condom. He kissed around my inner thigh and said,
"but I'm clean," his voice like dulce in my ear—I believed him, and he was.
The weeks of April and May will be full of all the impediments to love:
corporate trips he must take to Italy for weeks at a time; law school finals;
time he rightfully prioritizes with his cherub-children-of-elementary-
school-age (he has joint custody with his ex-wife, a corporate lawyer).
At the beginning of the summer, I will take myself to see the *Catholic
Imagination Exhibit* at the Cloisters. On that sunny day I'll write a sonnet
in the courtyard café about the Madonnina in Milan. It's veiled but it is
really just a poem about the first man who made me squirt.

HURSTON, ZORA NEALE. *THEIR EYES WERE WATCHING GOD.* PRINT.

Fresh off the Old Town trolley, I walk down King Street in Alexandria with so much confidence. It's the two-year anniversary (minus a three-month hiatus) of my first date with The Editor and we've been drinking at our favorite watering hole on King.

On this July night, we are both so intoxicated by one another and the spirits that he even "hypothetically" proposes to me. I say, "Yes," and we make out at the bar like teenagers would.[64] Later, walking back to his condo, he slowly begins to inch down the gold zipper on my corset-like top that extends from the dip of my cleavage to the waistband of my jean shorts. The corset's zipper breaks apart and I hand the whole thing to him. We then start a game of "Sexy Hansel and Gretel"—dropping "breadcrumbs"—taking off my strapless bra and tossing it to the ground, and then removing my jean shorts and letting them fall onto the concrete front steps of his condo. I then walk into the shared entrance lobby in just my birthday suit. In the morning I'll wake up with mosquito bites in the most novel places.[65]

. . . .

[64] For more on making out when you were a teenager, *see* **"Wharton, Edith."**

[65] For more stories about leaving your clothes behind like breadcrumbs, *see* **"Chopin, Kate."**

SCREAMING BLUE MESSIAH

Build:
1½ oz. Goldschlager
¼ oz. Blue Curacao
in a shot glass and light it on fire if you desire.

I am 16 years old and sitting quietly in my AP-US History course when my teacher tells the class I received the highest score on the unit test we took the week before—a 50 out of 50. Immediately, the "terrible twin" in my grade (who sits diagonally in front of me and received a 48) launches up out of her desk, turns back to face me, and spews in front of the entire class: "YOU got a 50?"

Her twin is much less terrible, nice in fact, but I've seen both scoop up awards like *Titanic* did in 1998. Both were taking geometry in 8th grade, while the rest of us were just getting our bearings in algebra. Terrible and Nice will even graduate first and second in the class, respectively, with Terrible going on to attend Harvard, and Nice—Stanford. I end up graduating seventh as the only Latina in the top 1 percent.

And in this moment, I am not "woke" enough to scream back: *Yeah! My dad can't read and my parents are barely educated—but I got a 50!* Instead, I stay quiet the way I always do, but the way she said "you" will stick somewhere in my brain for years to come.[66]

....
[66] Years later, you'll learn Terrible also went to law school and now works at a non-profit organization where she focuses on ending sex-based harassment in schools through know-your-rights education and litigation.

HUXLEY, ALDOUS. *BRAVE NEW WORLD.* PRINT.

In sixth grade you vote for Al Gore in the 2000 mock election because the Black child actor in your L.A. elementary school, the one from *The Little Rascals* remake that you saw the day it came out in 1994, tells you to. That child actor could have been your first boyfriend had your father never intervened.[67] He was the boy you first learned to flirt with at the back of the school bus. He was the boy who rode with you in your sister's new Mustang on select days after school. He was the boy who asked you to dance your first dance, during the "luau" in the cafeteria. But you have no other moves so he moves on to Flor, the other long-haired Latina in the class, and they hook up in a bush at a graduation party while Christina Aguilera, in the "Lady Marmalade" quartet, sings through the speakers.[68] And in seventh grade, it's a new campus and you hardly see him those first few weeks. And then 9/11 hits everyone on your twelfth birthday. Your family gets you an ice cream cake, but no one really feels like celebrating.

---

[67] *See also* **"Márquez, Gabriel García"** or *drink* **"Cane and Cola."**

[68] For more on the men in your life choosing the other long-haired Latina, *see also* **"Fitzgerald, F. Scott."**

LEWINSKY

In a Milkshake glass, add:
1 part Bailey's Irish Cream
1 part Southern Comfort
1 part Peppermint Schnapps
Garnish with a tower of Whipped Cream in concentric ovals
and the reddest strawberries you have.

I am 7 years old and parallel play with my Barbies at Laura's house. For not having any genitals, my Barbies are going at it pretty hard. Laura and I like to narrate the world our Barbies move through and sometimes our worlds intersect and no matter what, the scenario always ends in sex. Laura is narrating that her Barbies are "licking each other's assholes on top of the red Barbie mustang." She said she heard that in a movie her mother let her watch. It could have been *Twin Peaks* or *Jerry Maguire*. It's playdates like these that make me think I know what Clinton means when he says "sexual relations with that woman" when I watch him on the screen with my nanny or father after school.

IBSEN, HENRIK. *A DOLL'S HOUSE*. PRINT.

When your sister Karina was 16 she bought a dollhouse kit at Price Club (future Costco). She glue-gunned over the years when she could but never finished. She took the bones of the dollhouse with her when she married and moved in with her husband.

Now, her husband begins to disappear most nights to drink with his cop friends. One night, a mistress calls the house and makes herself known. Your brother-in-law Carlos tells your sister it only happened recently a few times. But your sister investigates and uses the number to pinpoint an address. With the address, she is able to Google Earth the mistress's home to see her husband's truck from four years ago parked safe and snug in the mistress's driveway.

After two children with her husband, a boy named Victor and a girl named Julissa, and after years of changing diapers and bringing extra-backups of clean clothes and getting them to school and museums and soccer practice and Dodger games and then cleaning each room, your sister's dollhouse gathers dust out in the garage.[69]

. . . .

[69] *Pair also with* **"Miscarriage"** *and take a shot of* **"Witch's Brew #2"** while you're at it.

DONNA REED

In a mixing glass over Ice, combine:
4 oz. Absolut Vodka
4 oz. Cranberry Juice
4 oz. Sour Mix
Strain into a chilled Old-Fashioned glass over a large Ice Cube
Garnish with a Grapefruit Twist.

I am 9 years old and I'm good at taking care of myself. Bus drops me off, I say bye to my best friend Cynthia, and I walk to an empty house and watch whatever channel I want and get my homework done under my own supervision. Sometimes I miss my nanny, my Martha #2, but my mami said she couldn't afford Martha #2 anymore and I said I understood. I either try to make my own dinner (quesadillas and French toast are my specialties) or wait for my papi to bring me leftovers from the restaurant where he cooks. My father goes to bed early and my mom gets home late. Sometimes I dread the sound of the garage door opening because that means she'll soon start screaming about how she's on her feet all day at the salon and that no one cares how hard she works.[70] She'll start watching her telenovelas after she tells me to bring her fuzzy pink pantuflas and put them on her feet. I'll try to tell her about my day at school but only during the commercials. If I talk during the telenovela she'll only "shush" me.[71]

....

[70] *Take a sip of* **"Horse and Jockey"** for more.

[71] *See also* **"Pink Panty Pulldowns"** for more on Martha #1.

IRVING, JOHN. *A PRAYER FOR OWEN MEANY.* PRINT.

Walking down the aisle of the church where my first communion was held almost twenty years before, I am so angry I could swat everyone's prayers away—it's also the church of my sister's quinceañera and my parents' 25th anniversary—*They will never make it to their golden anniversary now,* I think.

These thoughts had stewed while I was trapped in Ross: Dress for Less earlier that Saturday morning. The Saturday morning of my father's funeral—spent chauffeuring an aunt who came from Baja California for the funeral who neglected to bring anything black—my mother offers me up to take her to find something appropriate. There, I am trapped in the petites section surrounded by cheap fabric and discount prices while my father waits for us cold a few miles away. My tía tries on another outfit and I want to scream. With less than an hour to shower, I drive her back home at top speed.

In the church, I am wearing the black cocktail dress with the keyhole-lace back I also wore to my daddy's 70th birthday party—his final birthday party, though I did not know it at the time. Without a covering, another aunt tells me it is too provocative for a Saturday afternoon Mass. Near the altar, I slap on a black cardigan as if it were a leather jacket and I was in a biker gang. I walk down the aisle to meet my family and the priest at the entrance, walking as if there were a knife hidden in my black-leather Mary Jane heels, which I might use at any moment to cut a bitch. At the midpoint between the cross hanging over the altar and my mother crying over the closed coffin being wheeled in at the entrance, I turn around to stare at the cross. *This is some bullshit,* I whisper under my breath.

IMMACULADA

In a shaker half-filled with Ice Cubes, add:
½ oz. Light Rum
½ oz. Amaretto
½ oz. Lime Juice
1 tsp. Lemon Juice
and strain into a Goblet glass.

I am 28 years old and my dad tells me to get down on my rodillas at the entrance of the iglesia because he promised her.

Having heard my cries over the phone about how difficult my 2L is—how maybe I can't do it—my father took to praying to the Virgen de Talpa de Allende. The chaparrita.

My dad gets down first, using the pew to steady himself. His weak knees inch along the hard tile. I place my knees down and follow close behind him, up the aisle of the church, concentrating hard on his tennis shoes moving in front of me. My dad is wearing thick jeans, but I foolishly wore very thin leggings that day. I want to stand up and give up, but my dad is 70 and he is still pushing on. Not only that, but little old Mexican ladies in black veils on their wobbly knees are speeding past me. Somehow I make it and there she is—perfect in her little glass box, her pristine, little, beaded dress and her painted face. We meet my mom in a room adjacent to the altar. On a cement shelf built into the wall are offerings left behind: a diploma from a dental school in Guadalajara; bills for cancer treatment; trenzas in every shade of brown and black, cut off and offered. My mom whispers in my ear: "Those are for all the milagros people prayed for." I nod and promise my dad that if, and when, I finally graduate from law school, I'll bring my diploma and leave it for his chaparrita.[72]

. . . .

[72] **But will make sure to wear thicker pants or jeans next time.**

JACKSON, SHIRLEY. *THE HAUNTING OF HILL HOUSE*. PRINT.

The August before my third year of law school, I return to
California to console my mother in the months after my father's
death. The vastness of her California King lessens those nights,
as I take the side of the bed where my father's bodyprint remains.
Next to me, she prays the rosary every night at 10 pm and
cannot sleep without a sliver of light shining from the bathroom.
The drawers next to me are still filled with his socks, his white
undershirts, his watches, his bolo ties, his razors, his aftershave.
One night I dream I am in a coffee shop with my sister and my
niece. Out of the corner of my eye, I see my father in full cowboy
gear looking at us from the window. I run out to chase him but
the scenery changes from suburban Santa Clarita to a rancho in
Jalisco. He is walking on a dirt trail. I tell him to wait for me, but
he tells me I can't go where he is going; I need to turn back.[73] He
turns up a road and a metal gate closes behind him with a cruel
clang. "No me dejes papi," I scream out to him in agony. Back
on the California King, I feel someone hold my left hand in the
darkness. When I try to pull away, that someone grabs my wrist
lovingly and then holds my hand again. My mom is on my right,
and I am unable to reach her with my right hand. And when I
tell family members that last part, they think I was still dreaming.

....

[73] Yes, it is one of those dreams. So cliché and straightforward. You'll never quite
believe it until it happens to you.

CASA NOBLE (MARGARITA)

2 oz. Casa Noble Tequila Reposado
½ oz. Grand Marnier
1 oz. Fresh Lime Juice
Pour all ingredients over Ice
in a hand-painted clay jug and stir.

I am 8, 9, 10, 11, 12, 13, 14, 15, 16, 17, 18, 19, 20, 21, 22, 23, 24, 25, 27, 27, 28 and my daddy asks me, "Wouldn't you rather live in Mexico with all the ghosts?"

Your dad loves the house he bought his parents in Mexico but word among the primos is the place is legit haunted. It was built on a former panteón in the oldest part of the pueblo. Super poltergeist shit. You've never actually seen anything, but there are stories. When one of your cousins was a little girl, she pointed and told the adults around her that she could see an entire family eating in the house's garden courtyard. None of the adults could see them. One of your aunts once woke up standing in front of a dresser. She said she had seen blocks of gold reflected in the mirror and that something or someone had led her there. The house has large wooden doors that separate the outside from in but hanging sheet-curtains with 1970's prints divide all the actual bedrooms inside the house. As a little girl, you didn't like entering bedrooms by yourself. Sometimes you even found yourself ripping back the floral psychedelic print, almost wanting to see two ghostly Mexican girls in peasant dresses braiding each other's hair on top of your cobija san marcos just to prove your fears were justified. Instead, it's an empty room or, occasionally, just your dad holding his hands in the air like a bear with a "boo" or a little monster growl. You will scream and he will start chuckling very hard. Then he will tell you that even if there were ghosts, they would *never* hurt you.[74]

....

[74] For more on spirit-filled homes, *see also* **"Allende, Isabel."**

JAMES, HENRY. *THE PORTRAIT OF A LADY.* PRINT

Eyes. Hair. Breasts. Nose. Legs. Teeth. Face (overall). Brooke hands all the girls in the sleepover circle (of hell) these lists with each of our names on them so we can "rate" each other's beauty. One to ten. Everyone else seems to be getting high marks, especially Kelly (she looks like a Barbie) and Brittany (she looks like Angelina Jolie). My head is still reeling from truth-or-dare where I watched Brooke and Brittany make out (which was Brittany's first kiss) and now this. Some of the girls look like they gave me semi-high marks, which appear to be too high for Brooke. When she gets her hands on my sheet, she sighs heavily and tells the circle of girls, "Guys, you need to be more honest." Even though it was supposed to be "anonymous," I'm pretty sure Kimberley and Laura gave me lower marks after that, probably to stay in Brooke's good graces. It all feels like some Machiavellian betrayal and I'm not confident enough in my beauty yet to tell all those white girls that I'm digging the power of my gestalt.[75]

---

[75] For more stories about the whitest girls you know, drink **"Island Toy."**

JAMES THE SECOND COMES FIRST

In a mixing glass half-filled with Ice Cubes, combine:
2 oz. Scotch
½ oz. Tawny Port
½ oz. Dry Vermouth
Dash Bitters
Pour into a vintage Martini glass
That oozes with generational wealth.

I am 18 years old and a white boy who chooses to spell his name "Jaimz" (contrary to his birth certificate) whispers the worst sweet nothing into my ear: "It's okay that you got a full ride because you're not going to make any real money after you graduate."

We had been drinking in his dorm room late into the night and my roommate was not altogether fond of underage drinking, so he told me to stay and "take his bed." And, like a gentleman, he took the sleeping bag on the floor, at least for a bit.

I'm curled up in the fetal position with him nuzzling into my neck, and it makes sense why he asked what my first semester grades were (3.8 to his 3.9). Sadly, I'm not "woke" enough at this point in my life to school him on his privilege,[76] which includes but is not limited to parents who sent him to swim with tortoises in the Galapagos and track snow leopards in Russia when he was 16. Instead, I tell him to take back his bed and I'll take the floor. "It's okay," I assure him. "I'm used to it."[77]

. . . .

[76] For other times when you could have said more, *see also* **"Rand, Ayn"** or *sip* **"Screaming Blue Messiah."**

[77] For more on white people and scholarships, *see also* **"Twain, Mark."**

JOYCE, JAMES. A PORTRAIT OF THE ARTIST AS A YOUNG MAN. PRINT.

You've modeled so many college, graduate-school, law-school, and scholarship essays after this book, starting with "simple" language at the start and moving to more "complex" language by the end. You've shown countless panels, committees, and judges how you started off as a "moocow coming down along the road," and grown to a student, a woman who is able "to forge in the smithy of [her] soul the uncreated conscience of [her] race." Or you've tried to, at least. It's the kind of essay that inspires the Jesuits to give you a shit-ton of money to study. What's the catch? You recount stories of your largely illiterate father, the alcoholism in your family, a mother you rarely saw growing up. Stories of translating documents for your parents, writing letters to your mother's landlord when you're only 14, explaining that the rent increase for the beauty salon is too high and will be impossible for her to pay. Stories of helping your parents fill out important forms while no one is helping you complete your algebra. You have epiphanies in these essays about the reason you are so driven and so fiercely independent. This history is probably why you never ask for help, even when you absolutely need it.

WAKE THE DEAD

⅓ oz. *Bourbon Whiskey*
⅓ oz. *Green Chartreuse*
⅓ oz. *Sambuca*
Mix, serve, fall over and get back up again.

I am three years old and ask my father to read me a bedtime story. He tells me we have un problemón on our hands.

That night, I start reading my own fairy tales and my dad retreats to our salmon-colored leather couch to finish his two 24-packs of Budweisers. When I'm older I'll wonder about the reasons why he drank nearly 48 beers topped with Clamato juice every day during those years. Then, I'll remember that tiramisu I used to eat at his restaurant as a toddler. He was a co-owner, with his cousin Alejandro, of an Italian restaurant in Thousand Oaks but my dad was better with the food and Alejandro was the one skilled with the business.[78] Even though they both sported Pancho Villa moustaches, they could make Italian food like real Italians. Alejandro ended up selling the restaurant and didn't reimburse my father for all his investment money or his sweat. My mom begged my father to find a lawyer to make them whole, but my father refused. He only stopped speaking to his cousin. We had just moved to the house in Santa Clarita and my mom was really the only one who could put money towards the mortgage. So it was around this time my father began to fall asleep on the leather salmon-colored couch, surrounded by crushed beer cans, and there was no waking him after that.

. . . .

[78] For more on this son-of-a-bitch who is technically family, also *sip* **"Piedra Putamadre."**

KAFKA, FRANZ. *THE TRIAL.* PRINT.

1L: I receive grades I've never seen before. I don't talk to anyone in my section. My first cold call I speak softly and my argument fizzles into vapor. My 84-year-old male professor, the former president of the university, fills the lecture room of one hundred: "Confidence, Ms. Zapata. Lawyers say it with confidence." I cry every day. The constant beatdown normalizes during second semester until a wave ripples through law school community: A female alumnus—the first Black Muslim judge appointed to the state's court of appeals and associate judge of New York's highest court—found dead in the Hudson River. She was a trailblazer. She was smart. She was successful and in pursuit of a more just New York for all. My Gender Justice professor who knew her tells us all, almost in tears, that sometimes that's what imposter syndrome looks like. I nod and when people ask me how law school is going I almost say, *It can make you want to free fall until your fully clothed body is found floating near Harlem.* But I just tell them, "It's hard. It's so hard."

MILLIONAIRE SOUR (NON-ALCOHOLIC)

2 oz. Lemon Simple Syrup
2 oz. Ginger Ale
¼ cup Crushed Ice
¼ Shot Grenadine
Garnish with Lemon slices and at least 8 Cherries.

I am 27 years old and I am the soberest I've been in over ten years. The cold punch of the Socratic method requires it. Still, with all the small print, I can barely keep my vision straight anymore. In ConLaw I sit next to Abigail Birchmere Tellengard, a girl with two lawyer-parents whose idea of tough love is making her go straight through.[79] One morning I accidentally reach into her purse (which looks like mine, only the designer version). I realize my mistake and see her body gyrate uncomfortably in my periphery but neither of us says a word. Other mornings while I'm mid-text, she knocks my phone out of my hand with her backpack and never turns to me to say sorry. In Contracts, on the day we learn about *Bailey v. West*, the racing horse case, she is very knowledgeable about the price of keeping a horse. She looks like the kind of girl who would be. It's clear she had a father who poured his money into her horse. But my father poured his money into the races.[80]

. . . .

[79] You later learn she's Co-President of the Federalist Society and is of Cuban descent.

[80] *See also* **"McCarthy, Cormac"** and *sip* **"Horse and Jockey."**

KEROUAC, JACK. *ON THE ROAD.* PRINT.

There was nowhere to go but everywhere: except there wasn't, really. There we both were, trapped in a strip mall in Fresno with a McDonald's and Burlington Coat Factory and not much else. None of those mad people who explode like spiders across the sky in that town. When Cynthia, my best friend, told me she would be moving to San Francisco, I had offered to drive her that summer even though my mother told me not to.

And I lose control of the car going 85mph, car almost flips, but miraculously the car spins out and lands perpendicular to the road without hitting anyone. Still, the axle is fucked and AAA tows us to the strip mall for free. Cynthia and I take refuge in the Burlington Coat Factory for 8 hours, joking that Fresno is the purgatory of California, until my sister Karina and her husband Carlos come to save us. They come even though my sister is pregnant with their first kid. Her husband and his friend manage to hook up the car to tow it back to Santa Clarita but they tease us the whole time. "So how exactly did you Ricky Bobby the car? Cause the only thing that makes sense is that you two girls were zapping each other with vibrators and lost control," they say.

CALL A CAB

In a Highball glass with Ice,
Combine and stir:
¼ oz. Melon Liqueur
¼ oz. Peach Schnapps
¼ oz. Coconut Rum (Malibu)
¼ oz. Crème de Bananes
¼ oz. Vodka
¼ oz. Peach Liqueur
2½ oz. Cranberry Juice
Garnish with a Lemon spiral.

I am 24 years old and I am enjoying New Year's Eve at Next Door Lounge on La Brea with Cynthia.

It's not even midnight and we've lost track of the number of cocktails we've had. Two lonely men at the bar try to pick up the two drunkest girls in the room (that's us) and invite us to go dancing. My best friend doesn't shut it down like I expect and we take the bait. They drive us to a rave in downtown. It costs $100 dollars per person and the men offer to buy our tickets. We tell them a diner where we can talk might be better in that case, but they refuse to listen. After we finish dancing to the first song, we realize that for $400 dollars, they're going to want a hell of a lot more than the funky chicken. She and I lock eyes, we say we're going to the bathroom, and we run. We catch our breath in a parking lot where a lone man is doing tai chi across the length of the lot at 4am while we devise our plan. We know we left the car in North Hollywood and North Hollywood is nearly an hour away. We'll have to find some other means of transportation.

KUNDERA, MILAN. *THE UNBEARABLE LIGHTNESS OF BEING.* PRINT.

He doesn't always hold you the way you need so you compromise—you sprawl out naked on his bed and all his weight rests on top of you. You receive him like a sexy starfish, massage his temples, kiss his thirsty forehead, and scratch his head, the gray in his beard, his back. You dig your nails deep into its rough, varied, bulbous terrain while his sweet rescue dog chews a bone on the floor surrounded by piles of Harper's magazines and half-eaten socks. This man is only 12 years older than you and helps you reconcile your love of dirty old men—old but not too old.[81] He's an editor of Irish and Polish descent and loves words as much as you do and always offers you the perfect one from his little mental shop whenever you ask. You dig your nails deeper than you mean to and one of his boils bursts like balloon art down the canvas of his back. He runs to the bathroom. Without his weight, you pinch and smother his blood between your fingertips and know that this is love.

. . . .

[81] *See* **"Bukowsi, Charles"** and **"Nabokov, Vladimir Vladimirovich."**

DIRTY DR. SHOCKER

In a Collins glass with Ice, add:
3 oz. Dr. Pepper
½ oz. Coconut Syrup
Squeezed Lime 1 oz.
Aftershock
Stir only once.

I am 26 years old when I have my second one-night stand and it's nothing like the first.[82]

You only just met this man at a speakeasy near U and 14th. He suggests that you speakeasy-hop to another near 14th and U but not before he presses you against an underground staircase and kisses you. Hard. It's borderline assault but you roll with it because you're so numb from your recent break-up with The Editor. This is the first man you've slept with who has a PhD. He's 40. He works at the US Treasury and has special clearance. As if it isn't nauseatingly DC enough, he tells you he lives around the corner and across the street from your favorite Supreme Court Justice. The house he owns was built during the Civil War and slants slightly and his dick is so small you barely feel it, at least. In the morning, you take a strumpet stroll after staring at the Supreme Court Justice's stylish apartment building at least that's how you brush it off later to your roommate. But at the time, it doesn't feel like a strumpet stroll. It doesn't really feel like anything.

. . . .
[82] *See also* **"Austen, Jane."**

LAWRENCE, D.H. *SONS AND LOVERS*. PRINT.

At dinner with my family, a bowl of carne asada and beans flies past my four-year old head and paints the white wall behind me. The moment the bowl crashes to the floor, my older sister grabs me by my little torso and carries me up the stairs, like we're fleeing a battle. Safe on the second floor, my sister and I watch as our father and brother exchange punch after punch all the way into the foyer. My mother is crying and pleading that they stop fighting, stop punching. For years, I'll think this impromptu boxing match began because my older brother told my parents he had recently married his high school girlfriend without telling them. I ask my older sister to confirm this after my graduation and she says even though our brother Nacho got married in secret around that same time, the fight in question began because my brother wanted a tattoo and my dad thought it was disrespectful of him to want one.[83]

. . . .

[83] For more tales involving those quality family dinners, *also sip* some **"Screaming Pornstar."**

PAPA DOBLE

Combine and strain into a Martini glass:
1 shot White Rum
1 Shot Rose's Sweetened Lime Juice
1 Shot Grapefruit Juice
Ice
Garnish with 1 Lime wedge.

I am 5 years old and I run down the stairs yelling, "papi papi papi papi, papi," the entire way and jump into my father's arms the second he gets home from work.

I sit in his checkered-pants lap, kiss his bandaged fingers, poke the grease stains on his uniform, and twirl the ends of his Pancho Villa moustache.[84] I sing him songs I learned in kindergarten that day. He sweetly calls me his "sapo," his "sope de perro," his "prieta." Cause I'm the baby and he loves me. My older brother Nacho and older sister Karina may have experienced Old Testament Jesus in the 80s, but it's the 90s now and I get New Testament Jesus through and through.

It's around this time I learn I have a half-brother David who lives in Omaha and a half-sister Ana who lives in Inglewood. They call on my dad's birthday and he calls them on their birthdays. Eventually, I'll meet them, these children from other mothers. And when I do and I see their faces, as my papi scoops me into his arms, I'll feel guilty I'm one of the children my daddy chose to raise.

....

[84] The Pancho Villa mustache may have been shaved off in later years but even in your 20s so much of this stays the same.

LEE, HARPER. *TO KILL A MOCKINGBIRD.* PRINT.

Riding my bike through the neighborhood and down the hill without a helmet and no hands on the handlebar, it's no surprise that I wake up in the hospital with a concussion however many hours later.

That day, I had intended play with my sixth-grade friend Giselle, but Kimberley told me to cancel because I would be riding bikes that day with *her*.[85] No hands on the handlebar was a move she "invented" and called "the freefall" and I have to do it, too. But at the bottom of the hill I see Giselle playing in the grass next to a tree with Cynthia, my best friend, the way *I* was supposed to—and then the memory cuts. I'm told there was a ditch in the road, I flew into the air, landed on the pavement and convulsed violently, and had to take a $1200 ambulance ride my family could not afford. With the emergency room bill the total came to $4000, and we had no medical insurance.

My mom hires a personal injury lawyer to sue the construction company who was building new tract homes in the neighborhood and created the ditch in the first place. Two years later, the construction company pays for our medical bills and gives me an extra grand I'll get when I turn 18. I don't remember what I used the money for, but I'll never forget my mom and sister having to wake me up every three hours the night of the accident to shove blue pills up my butt to make sure I didn't go into a coma and climb out of my skin.

. . . .

[85] *See also* **"Golding, William"** for this girl and her reign of terror.

TEQUILA MOCKINGBIRD

In a shot glass:
1 oz. Tequila
1 Lime
Garnish with 1 Blackberry Pink-Peppercorn Shrub.

I am 8 years old and folding my mom's white salon towels on the long, leather, salmon couch and putting them in three piles. My Dad is on the loveseat folding his pile.

It's Saturday and he woke me up at 7am so I can fold the toallas for my mom's beauty salon with him and watch *Plaza Sésamo* until they're all done. In this little family sweatshop, this was my sister's job before me and my brother's job before her. My dad will take them out of the dryer and dump them where they land hot on the couch cushion. Sometimes the white piles of towels tower over me and, like Cinderella, I never know when I'll get through them all. It feels like I never will.

Having done it for two decades, my dad finishes his pile first and then makes my mom lunch. When I am done, Kimberley will usually call me to play and we will spend the rest of our Saturday climbing across the hills behind our houses, avoiding rattlesnakes, and looking into our neighbor's backyards and pools along the way.

LONDON, JACK. *WHITE FANG.* PRINT.

The first time I have sex with The Editor his dog is watching from the corner of the room. It's hard to concentrate on blowing him. I want to ask if I can tell the dog to go to the living room but have a feeling the border collie mix is the real master of the condo. With time, I'll notice the dog less during sex, and the fact that he jumps on the bed for pets after we're done only adds to all the love. We will all spend my first official east coast blizzard holed up in the condo together. The Editor will have passed the "blizzard test" with flying colors while the other blue-eyed gentleman I've also been dating,[86] who wanted to Netflix-and-Chill by himself, failed miserably.[87] The Editor and I walk mitten in glove through the snow to the empty restaurants open on King Street, drinking Mexican Hot Chocolate—vanilla, almond, Abuelita chocolate, mezcal and chantilly cream.[88] Old Town will be silent and still covered in all the snow, with a hint of diesel from the trucks clearing and salting the roads. When we get back to the condo, I'll have no problem shoveling snow off the sidewalk so that the dog can piss and do his business because I love that border collie mix so much.

. . . .

[86] *See also* **"Brontë, Charlotte."**

[87] *See also* **"Stevenson, Robert Louis."**

[88] For King Street in the summertime, *see also* **"Hurston, Nora Zeale."**

HAIR OF THE DOG

In a red plastic cup, add:
½ oz. Irish Whiskey
½ oz. Tequila
¼ oz. Tabasco Sauce
¼ oz. Salt
Garnish with 1 Jalapeño for extra kick in the behind.

I am 24 years old and my brother-in-law hands me this cocktail to revive me.

A crumpled pile of flesh in the passenger seat of their Tahoe, you're hungover in Big Bear from drinking every variety of German beer the wenches offered you at Oktoberfest. Not only that, high elevations always make you sick. And the night before, you had convinced your brother-in-law's sister and her boyfriend to put you in the trunk on the ride back to the cabin, like in the movie *The Hangover*. You'll later watch your brother-in-law have a snowball fight with his son Victor, while your sister has their 6-month-old daughter Julissa strapped to her chest. The memory of watching your brother-in-law play and laugh with Victor in the snow will only become tarnished when you learn this is around the time he found his mistress.[89]

After that, all those times he saved you and saved your sister won't matter to you anymore.

....

[89] *See also* **"Ibsen, Henrik."**

LORDE, AUDRE. ZAMI: *A NEW SPELLING OF MY NAME*. PRINT.

I re-name myself Mónica when I am a toddler, against my mother's wishes. I tell my mother, with attitude, to call me Mónica. I tell all my tíos and tías and even strangers I meet in stores to call me Mónica. I re-name myself because my stubborn 2 ½-year-old mind already knows what I officially become cognizant of when I turn 5 and find my birth certificate: that my mom learned to hate the name she originally gave me and legally changed it in a San Fernando Valley courthouse. The story goes that my Tía Sandra, who lives in Ensenada, said "Valentina" was the name of the poor beggar woman who sold bread in our pueblo in Mexico. How could she name a baby that? And "Carmina," the middle name, was for my mom's mother, but that had to be changed too.[90] There's a home video of my sister and primas recording themselves. For a few seconds, they pan over to the baby in the crib and don't know what to call her. But when I become a toddler, I know exactly what to call her.[91]

....

[90] *See also* "**Woolf, Virginia.**"

[91] To this day, when your Tío Memo sees you, he calls out, "Dónde está mi Mónica?" Then, he'll scrunch his face the way he says *you* did when you were a toddler, and sputter out "Mónica" the way he says you used to do, his laughs filling up a room.

LICK-HER-ITCH

Combine and shake with Ice:
½ oz. Sambuca
1 oz. Vodka
½ oz. Cranberry Juice
Strain into a shooter. Garnish with
1 Cherry.

I am 27 years old and my boyfriend The Editor writes to a girl in my voice and on my account, using the OKCupid app on his phone.

Her username is "Wu-tang Clams" and she likes puns, British rom-coms, Elliott Smith, intersectionality, Frida Kahlo, loves writing in coffee shops, is studying for the LSAT, and lives in Brooklyn.
"I think you'll like her," The Editor tells you.
"Hook it up, Cyrano," you tell him while rubbing his dog's belly. You and The Editor both decided long ago that you have an open relationship—he gets only you, but you can have a chica every now and then. In Washington, DC you have your man and in New York you have as many women your awkward self can handle. You have these parameters as part of your long-distance relationship because you don't want to get married to him one day and then finger some girl under the table because you didn't adequately explore that part of your sexuality.[92]

....

[92] For more fingering under the table, *sip* **"Silk Panties with Lace."** And you will never marry him. *See also* **"Waugh, Evelyn."**

MARTEL, YANN. *LIFE OF PI.* PRINT.

Summing up my father's life is too much. I've always been praised for my writing but whatever I type in the Word doc would never do him justice, and I say that. Writing it in Spanish and spilling tequila on my desk, I say, "he was not a man who can be described en pocos párrafos," but that feels cliché. Like those blind men and the elephant, my daddy was certainly a different man to different people—even a different man to each of his children.[93] I write that my father started off in America as a meat packer in Nebraska, then became a factory worker in Newhall, and then a cook. He was a man of service, among other things. Through blurry eyes, I finish the rest of the obituary and email it to my sister who requested it, telling her I can't look at it anymore. My brother reads what I wrote during the rosary service, and I thought that was that. But during the mass two days later the priest looks down and proclaims that now I will read some words I wrote about my father. My spacey sister forgot to tell me about this detail.[94] After a game of hot potato in the front of pew—passing our brother's iPhone between the siblings with the Word doc on it, I find the confidence, walk past the coffin, and address all the pews filled with teary-eyed people. I start with his death, then his birth, his parents, the wife he loved, the children he had. He always told me he wasn't smart. But I know that a boy who crossed a border by himself and then made a life in America *did* have brains. I let this line ring in the church, his body no longer able to protest: "El era un hombre *tan* inteligente." Because he was. He really was.

. . . .

[93] *Also gulp down* **"Papa Doble."**

[94] And it's not like I even practiced reading it like I otherwise would have because I was trapped in a Ross: Dress for Less that morning. *See* **"Irving, John."**

WORKING MAN'S ZINFANDEL

In a beer mug with Crushed Ice,
Add:
1 shot Tequila
1 Shot Scotch
½ Shot Cinnamon Schnapps
½ Shot Peach Schnapps
Gulp down.

I am 3, 4, 5, 6, 7, 8, 9, 10, 11, 12, 13, 14, 15, 16, 17, 18, 19, 20, 21, 22, 23, 24, 25, 27, 27, 28 years old and eating the most delicious food prepared by my father's hands.[95]

My daddy always woke up at dawn, and usually had a whole feast prepared in our suburban kitchen while the rest of us were still snoring above. Five-star meals made in a three-star kitchen and zero-star garage. Almost Rumplestiltskin-style, he could transform boxes from Smart & Final and packages of bloody meat into the most decadent and delicious buffet you could find—for parties of every kind. His hands always expertly cutting chicken into cubes, removing the fat, and mixing the flesh with his secret marinade—a squishy sound. A true artist in the kitchen, he was not always the best negotiator and practically gave the food away sometimes, worried about where it was prepared even though your mom always assured him no one could tell.

Even in a Mariachi song a friend of your father's will write for him some day, the lyrics will read that your father tended to slave away even when he wasn't paid very much.

....

[95] For more on your father's food, *also sip* **"Alien Urine Sample."**

MÁRQUEZ, GABRIEL GARCÍA. *ONE HUNDRED YEARS OF SOLITUDE / CIEN AÑOS DE SOLEDAD.* PRINT.

Many years later, as I faced the firing squad of my family, I was to remember that distant afternoon past when my father took me to purchase ice at Tresierras. Tresierras was the Hispanic supermarket on the "Mexican" side of town. I was in the checkout line with my father when a little boy from my kindergarten class waved at me and yelled my name from across the store. I froze. I ignored him. I refused to look in his direction. Though she wasn't even there, my mother pins this as the moment when I became ashamed of my heritage.[96] But I refused to wave not because Manuel was Mexican but because he was a boy, and my Dad, tired of all my older sister's suitors, told me he would hang any boyfriend I ever had in his walk-in closet on a wire hanger. I didn't have my first boyfriend until I was 22. There are just certain things you shouldn't say to a 4-year-old girl.

. . . .

[96] *See also* **"Shakespeare, William."**

TIGHT SNATCH

Shake with Ice:
½ oz. Vodka
½ oz. Peach Schnapps
1 oz. Orange Juice
1 oz. Cranberry Juice
Pour into a cocktail glass of your choosing over more Ice.

I am 19 years old and I am the youngest person in my "Roadwrite" class. Our professor has taken us on the road up to Big Sur to inspire our writing and we're staying at a motel across the way from elephant seals humping on the beach.

The senior girl I was assigned to share a bed with, decides to hook up with the gorilla-esque yet thoughtful jock in the class but regrets it midway through and rolls over. It's Valentine's Day. I've been relegated to the floor with the butch lesbian and the sleeping bag she offered me. The jock attempts to clandestinely jack off under the sheets, but not even the snores of my floormate, the drunk hiccups of the two girls in the other queen bed, or the elephant seals humping on the coast can mask that rustling.

MARX, KARL. *THE COMMUNIST MANIFESTO.* PRINT.

In the hair-salon community there are no secrets. Your mother routinely tells her entire life story and yours to each and every one of her clients. She even asks them for advice about your life. She'll call you at home and say So-and-So wants to speak to you. Who's So-and-So? But before you even get an answer, you're on the phone for five minutes or more, with So-and-So either saying how proud they are of you or telling you what major you should choose or what law school you should choose or what city you should live in. And whenever you visit the salon in person, you'll meet someone you have never seen before who practically knows everything about you. Their face will light up when you try to introduce yourself. But they need no introduction because they know exactly who you are.

RED ALERT

Vigorously shake:
1½ oz. Tequila (White)
1½ oz. Banana Liqueur
1 oz. Sloe Gin
Fill with Sweet and Sour and
Garnish with a bitter Lemon. The whole damn thing.

I am 28 years old and The Russian man in his late 30s pulls my bloody tampon out and throws it down on his wood floor—seductively.

This confuses you because when you walked into his apartment in Midtown, he reprimanded you for not taking your boots off by the door. It is a first date. You met on *Tinder*, his name is Dimitri, and he looks like a physically fit Rasputin. But you're still in post-break-up feast phase so you're up for whatever.[97] Drinking: check, always. Smoking marijuana: something you've only done once, but fine, whatever.[98] Check. However, you have your period. "So at most we can make out," you tell him. But it's not a deal breaker for him. And you spend many more hours there than anyone ever should. He tells you that you can stand to lose a few pounds.

He makes a comment about how fast you inhaled the takeout sushi he bought you. And when you turn to discuss film (you bring up *Eyes Wide Shut*) he tells you: "That movie is pure trash."[99] You tell him you've never heard a Kubrick film described that way. He then does a cheeched-out brain explosion and explains he thought you meant *50 Shades of Gray*.

Later, a friend will ask how you felt the moment the tampon was ripped out of you. "95% violated and 5% aroused," you'll say. But in the light of day, that will feel like 5 percent too much.

. . . .

[97] *See also* **"McCullers, Carson."**

[98] *Sip* **"Puff's Magick Dragon."**

[99] To see how your Kubrick knowledge is supposed to go when you are opposite a decent man, *see* **"Burgess, Anthony."**

MAUGHAM, W. SOMERSET. *OF HUMAN BONDAGE.* PRINT.

As little girls in elementary school, me and my white childhood friends—Kimberley, Laura, and Cynthia—loved tying each other to my bedposts with my mom's pretty scarves. Tucked away in a drawer in the jacuzzi room, she had scarves she never wore in every color and texture. We would take a bright fuchsia one and wrap it tight around Cynthia's white wrists. We would take one with a dreamy Parisian setting and blindfold Laura's big blue eyes. We would take a soft ebony one and cover Kimberley's mouth. They would take a lush red one so they could bind my feet. One girl would be left in the room and others would close the door and giggle outside, timing each other to see who could remove their velvety chains the fastest. In high school, we all mention these antics to one of the senior boys we are hanging out with and he suggests we time him after school to see how fast he can get out. My sister Karina comes home from work and finds a seventeen-year-old boy gagged, bound, and tied to my bed's headboard. Karina promises she won't tell my mom but says I have to be her slave.[100]

---

[100] For more on being your older sister's slave, *sip* **"Beetlejuice."**

MEXICAN THANKSGIVING

Combine in a shooter:
¾ oz. Tequila
¾ oz. Wild Turkey 80 Proof Bourbon
1 tbsp. Tabasco Sauce
Garnish with a Red Chili Pepper.

I am 3 years old and staunchly refuse to wear the emerald-green dress with the silky sash my mom has laid out on my bed for the Thanksgiving party.

It's also my dad's birthday and he's been preparing the food all morning and the house smells so delicious I can basically swallow a huge helping of the air. Frustrated with my screams and stomping, my mom threatens to bring my dad into the room to convince me with "his amigo," the leather belt. Knowing I'm his favorite and his little girl, I take her bluff. But he takes her side and spanks me so hard with his amigo I retreat underneath my bed for the rest of the party. My sister and my nanny (Martha #1) will come to my room and convince me to put the dress on and come downstairs, even bringing me scraps of turkey, despite my dad's warning not to give me dinner. I'll hear so much laughter, snippets of Spanish, and even Mariachi playing downstairs. Then my mom will come to the room, place her hand underneath the bed to pet my hair, and tell me that all my tías and tíos want to see me. I bite her fingers and tell her they'll have to come upstairs to see me.

MCCARTHY, CORMAC. *ALL THE PRETTY HORSES.* PRINT.

In America, I watch the jockeys at the racetrack make the pretty horses trot and gallop. In Mexico, I see my father can get on a horse and make the horse trot, gallop, and even dance to the tune of the banda playing in the pueblo's plaza. And in America, I don't ask too many questions when he tells me he needs me to fill out a withdrawal slip: name, date, address, and savings account number he has written on a paper he keeps in his wallet and hands to me. I want to tell him "no" or even rip up the slip, especially when he tells me to leave the amount "empty" for him to fill. It's because every move of the pen feels like one of these magnificent beasts trotting on my heart and on my mother's heart. But he's my father and he can't write anything more than his signature and a few numbers, so I can't tell him no.

TRAILER WENCH

1 Jigger Midori Melon Liqueur
1 Jigger Vodka
1 Jigger 151 Proof Rum
Fill with Grape Juice
Serve in a jelly glass with a swizzle stick.

I am 5 years old and my mom takes me to visit her father and his wife in the trailer home where they live in Canyon Country.

After my mom's mom, the grandmother I was once named for, after she died or disappeared when my mom was 5 years old, my Abuelo Pedro started a new family and left his 12 children to fend for themselves. My mom was traded and tossed between whatever aunts or uncles could take her until she came to America when she was 16.

Here, my grandfather is in his 80's and my mom's stepmother is in her late 50's and wheels him around the trailer. Before we got there, my mom explained what a "madrastra" is—Spanish for stepmother that sits heavy on my tongue. My mom has brought her father plaid shirts she picked up from Mervyn's so he can stay warm in the California winter. In the car she told me she only has a few memories of him. When she was a little girl, he would put flour on her nose and just laugh. He once shot a dog she loved. He always smelled of cerveza. I sit down on their worn couch and my Abuelo doesn't recognize my mom. He has Alzheimer's and has the luxury of leaving everything in the past.

MCCULLERS, CARSON. *THE HEART IS A LONELY HUNTER*. PRINT.

You and the Editor—the man you had hoped you would marry—have broken up for the second and final time, it seems.[101] So, you take to *Tinder* and start feasting on New York City like the human buffet that it is. And any helping that helps you avoid your Administrative Law reading is a bonus: a Jewish lawyer who fingers you against the floor-to-ceiling window of his multi-million-dollar apartment with views of Midtown. A hipster hairstylist in Bed-Stuy who takes you bowling in Brooklyn and then pins you playfully across the street from Biggie's childhood playground. A Ukrainian comedian in Hell's Kitchen who you sucked off once and never finished watching *A Few Good Men* with. Another Jewish lawyer—a tax lawyer—who moonlights as an extra at The Met Opera, invites you over to Netflix-and-Chill but opens the door of his Upper West Side studio apartment wearing his pajamas and somehow expects you to swoon. And even a tall, dark, and handsome architect in Chelsea that made your vagina queef very, very loud and long, to the horror of his posh lodgings.

....

[101] For more on The Editor *see also* **"Hurston, Zora Neale"** or **"Kundera, Milan"** or **"London, Jack"** or **"Waugh, Evelyn."** And *take a gulp of* **"Cold War."**

CREAMY PUNANI

Fill a blender ¾ full with Vanilla Ice-Cream then add:
2 oz. Kahlua
oz. Amaretto
3 oz. Bailey's Irish Cream
Blend until real smooth.

I am 28 years old and it is the year of allowing three special men to cum inside me: the Jewish Black guy from Harlem,[102] The Italian on the Upper East Side,[103] and even the Irish-Polish ex[104] from D.C. comes into the mix—again and against my better judgment.

Thank goodness you opted for that intrauterine device during your first year of law school, the insertion of which almost led you to collapse in pain on a homeless man on a cold day after emerging from the innards of the Planned Parenthood on Bleecker Street. But that's in the past and it is a hot summer when you realize that these three men who have served you some hefty cream pies have done so in pretty close succession. You get tested regularly and so do they but you get paranoid (especially when you can't feel the strings) whether that little plastic contraption floating inside you is still doing its job. You tell your sister on the phone one Saturday that you felt nauseous around midday. She tells you that you better not be, you know. You tell her: "That would be a nightmare—it would be like an episode of *Maury* or *Montel* over here."[105]

. . . .

[102] *See also* **"Ellison, Ralph."**

[103] *See also* **"Burgess, Anthony."**

[104] *See also* **"Kundera, Milan."**

[105] And for more cum concerns, *see also* **"Williams, Tennessee"** or *gulp down* **"Bloated Bag of Monkey Spunk."**

MELVILLE, HERMAN. *MOBY DICK.* PRINT.

In Los Angeles, that skinny white boy from Buffalo, New York with the funny accent was always my white whale.[106] In Los Angeles, all I wanted was for him to call me and invite me to his comedy shows in Hollywood, but I had to settle for stalking his *Facebook* page instead. But in Washington, D.C., years later, I caught him. When he tells me he's coming to town for some comedy shows, I have no problem offering up my couch, even though I haven't seen him in over five years. I go to his shows in Dupont Circle and Columbia Heights, then watch the fourth season of *American Horror Story* comfortably in my bed with him and my roommate. He'll come to town again months later en route to New Orleans and ask if I want to meet. I'll buy him brussels sprouts on H Street because I know he has less than five dollars in his bank account. He'll tell stories about a red-haired girl who broke his heart (they do that), his newfound sobriety, wild nights he spent with a C-list comedian and serious phone calls to his best friend, an MTV VJ from the 1990s. After I see him off at Union Station, he'll call to say his bus is delayed and asks if I want to come back. I'll tell him I can't. It was fun but I'm too tired and have to teach the next day.

....

[106] *See also* **"Fitzgerald, F. Scott"** and **"Rhys, Jean."**

BLOATED BAG OF MONKEY SPUNK

Shake and strain:
1 oz. Rum (Bacardi)
1 oz. Peach Schnapps
½ oz. Grand Marnier
1 oz. Pineapple Juice
Pour carefully into your back-up flask.

I am 26 years old and swallow Plan B on King Street after a sleepless night.

You have health insurance now (thanks, Obama) and yet, your only form of protection is still the pull-out method. You and The Editor have survived a breakup[107] and the chlamydia that you gave him[108] and you're back in the saddle again screwing like animals. Equal parts sultry and clumsy around him, you spilled rum and coke on his computer and felt so guilty, you got extra slutty in the bedroom. When you tell him to take you from the back, it doesn't work but he's so drunk and it's 4am that he thinks it is the back door and so, he cums.

At 8am, he hands you the CVS bag and plays you some song in the car about a girl who says "Make-Believe" but the boy hears "Maple Leaves."

. . . .

[107] *Take a gulp of* **"Cold War."**

[108] *Sip* **"Feel the Burn."**

MILLER, ARTHUR. *THE CRUCIBLE.* PRINT.

Because graduate school problematizes everything. I moved
out on her and suddenly my other "friends" in the program now
look at me as if I were dancing in the woods with the Devil.[109]
I should have ditched them a long time ago, really. Even when
they were my "friends" those white girls who married Latino
men never missed an opportunity to make me feel that I wasn't
"Mexican" enough. The Jewish one, who sometimes wears
traditional dresses she brags she haggled for in Oaxaca, tells
me how she and her Mexican husband often joke and call me a
pocha. Still, she never takes the time to tease out the complexities
of traumatic assimilation or consider how I got a full scholarship
to a literature program because my parents barely speak English.
I'm learning with the help of post-colonial theory that race is
nothing but a construct but my whole life white girls made me
feel like I wasn't "white" enough so this new development is some
bullshit.[110]

---

[109] *See* **"Díaz, Junot."**

[110] *See* **"James, Henry," "Shakespeare, William,"** and *take a sip of* **"Island Toy."**

WITCH'S BREW #2

Mix in a mini-cauldron with Ice:
2 oz. Yellow Chartreuse
1½ oz. Blue Curacao
½ oz. Brandy, spiced
Add ¼ tsp. Ground cloves
Stir, then get ready for double, double toil and trouble.

I am 22 years old, and my sister Karina invites me to a Halloween Party in the Hollywood Hills.

You don't want to go but your mom urges you because you've been sitting in your pajamas all day and seem depressed.[111] You're probably also upset about a combination of #1 (*see* Fitzgerald, F. Scott), #2 (*see* Hawthorne, Nathaniel) and #3 (*see* Austen, Jane). You recycle your "sexy" pirate costume from two years ago. Your sister is dressed as a self-proclaimed slutty peacock, a paradox that belongs at the Playboy mansion she looks so good. You drink the perpetual mystery punch from the black cauldron and don't talk to many people until 3am when the punch makes you very chatty with a Spartan. He frenches and fingers you on top of a speaker for the remaining partygoers to see (which include your brother-in-law and his friend, a heavy-set male Latino dressed as a Hooter's girl who rescues you). You cry on the car ride home to your sister's. When you get there, your brother-in-law Carlos (who was dressed as Santa Claus) comes out of the bedroom naked and you immediately throw the mystery punch up in the sink. Your sister, Karina, screams at her husband to put on some clothes because his naked body is making her little sister vomit.

. . . .

[111] *See also* **"Plath, Sylvia."**

MILTON, JOHN. *PARADISE LOST.* PRINT.

As a little girl, the garden courtyard in your grandparent's house in Mexico was your playground and your Eden.[112] After they passed, they left the main house to your father, who had bought them the entire property, and the corral to all the daughters. Through a series of deaths and bad finances, four daughters are written out, and the eldest daughter Renalda ends up owning the entire corral, which she immediately builds houses on. A communal door links the main house and the apartments. Once your father passes, Renalda changes the locks to the communal door and tells your father's childhood friend who watches over the main house that she blames your mother for your father's death. That it wasn't your father's time. That all your mother did was give him a heartburn pill. That your mother could have done more. Because it's a small town, y la gente habla,[113] the rumor that your mother killed your father spreads like wildfire by the time your family comes for your father's second funeral Mass in Mexico. You already spend your days assuring your mother that it wasn't her fault, and now this? From familia? Feeling like you and your relatives are trapped in a Mexican telenovela, the priest at the funeral mass in Tenamaxtlán becomes the saving grace, aware of all the town chisme. He tells everyone seated in that church—scolds them even—that "God decides when it's time. We do not get to decide when someone's time is up." You shoot a meaningful glance at your Tía Renalda and hold your mother's hand tightly.

....

[112] For more on the house in Tenamaxtlán *sip* **"Casa Noble"** or **"Pooky and Chooky."**

[113] For more on this talkative town in Mexico, also *sip* **"Horny Mohican."**

PIEDRA PUTAMADRE

½ oz. Tequila (Herradura Reposado)
½ oz. Fernet Branca
½ oz. Anisette (Cadenas)
Garnish with plenty of Jalapeño slices.

I am almost 29 years old and my father's archenemy, his cousin Alejandro,[114] has the cojones to come to my father's funeral service in Mexico.

My father took his painful grudge to the grave and, as my father's daughter, I have no problem carrying his legacy. Preoccupied with walking my mother down to the church aisle, however, all I can do is shoot him the nastiest look because I do not have a poker face. But what I really want is to throw a rock at my Tío Alejandro's head, rip the creepy Pancho Villa mustache he still sports off his face, and bounce him out of the Lord's House, reminding him that showing up to the funeral service doesn't mean he's forgiven. He is not forgiven, by me at least, for robbing my father, his family, of thousands upon thousands of dollars and stripping my father of his spirit in the early 1990s over a restaurant. My sister Karina, however, who is as sweet as can be and remembers good times with Tío Alejandro in the 1980s before I was born, can be found crying in his arms after the Mass. She tries to call me over but I refuse. Later, my older prima Julieta suggests that maybe now, more than ever, it's time to forgive. I look down into my plastic cup of Johnnie Walker Red and tell her I'm just too angry to forgive.

· ·

[114] *Also sip* **"Wake the Dead."**

MITCHELL, MARGARET. *GONE WITH THE WIND.* PRINT.

"I don't mind if they get together and have sex but they just can't get married," my mother tells me when I am seated in passenger seat of the Lincoln Navigator on the way to church. I had just watched Salma Hayek play the role of "Frida" the night before and there was something about Diego coming out of the revolving door of the hotel with a different woman every night that made me want to roll my eyes. But when Frida comes out of the hotel in her traditional Mexican dresses onto the New York streets with a woman she later puts her hands on underneath the table in the diner, I felt something, and it scared me. This is also the era when I am surrounded by white pre-teen girls who hit their computer when it's acting "gay" and call each other a derogatory word for lesbian they made up: *llstevers*. "They can't get married? Like your marriage is so perfect," I roar at my mother. After that, I muster all the gumption I have, to jump out of the car when it's still in motion, because I refuse to hear my mom talk that way about marriage.[115]

. . . .

[115] Years later, there will be a weekend when you are studying for the LSAT, and your mother will ask you if you want to go to a wedding with her. It will be for one of her employees in Malibu, Armando, who is marrying his boyfriend. You'll smile, tell her you'd love to, but you have to study, and you're glad she's going.

PINK PANTY DROPPER

Fill punch bowl with Ice
Add:
12 can(s) Beer
½ Gallon(s) Vodka
7 cans(s) Pink Lemonade
Garnish with Lemon wheel slices,
after beer stops foaming,
if desired.

I am 25 years old, holding two bottles of wine and two cases of beer, when my lace panties slowly inch past knees and plop in the dairy aisle in Safeway.

I whisper to the friend I came with, asking her to "cover" me. We had offered to pick up some alcohol before we went to the BBQ in Petworth. She covers me but can't believe what I have just told her. With all that alcohol, I am somehow able to maneuver into a feminine squat and horseshoe the panties on my foot, ball them discreetly into my palm, and toss them into my purse.[116] So much of my money went into liquor and not laundry in those days and that had been my last "good" pair, even if the elastic wasn't my friend. In the checkout line, my friend can't stop laughing because she feels trapped in an episode of Broad City. On the way to Petworth, she reminds me not to get my pussy lips on her passenger seat. When we get to the BBQ, she tells everyone there about the Safeway episode. I'll turn redder than the wine I'm holding because most of the guests are second-year men from our English program, including The Teaching Assistant [117]

....

[116] And for more on pink panties, *sip* **"Pink Panty Pulldowns"** and for when it comes to putting on your big girl chonies, *gulp* **"Feel the Burn."**

[117] *See also* **"Queirós, Eça de."**

MORRISON, TONI. *BELOVED*. PRINT.

When my high school English teacher sliced up the title and main setting of this book with chalk, I knew I was hooked on books. "124 was spiteful" and the novel was filled with a blues/tone that made Sethe the bluest/one, but by the end she told me to be/loved and not to be haunted by my nightmares. This is exactly what I needed to hear my senior year of high school when I had no friends after the car accident that left me traumatized. This novel taught me empathy and the importance of looking outside myself, the importance of understanding pain and trauma, not merely my own.[118]

------

[118] When you attended Toni Morrison's book signing in Washington, DC on April 30, 2015, I hope you didn't make a fool of yourself. *See also* **"Eugenides, Jeffrey."**

SEXUAL HEALING

In a Collins glass:
1 oz. Amaretto
1 oz. Kahlua
½ oz. Peppermint Schnapps
2 oz. Milk
Stir sensually . . . all night long.

I am 22 years old and upset with my first and then boyfriend, Pablo. My father sits down on my bed and wipes away my tears with his rough thumbs. He tells me a (his)story.

In the 1970s when he was 26 and my mother was 21, he would take her out every other night on dates, winning over not only my mother, but her aunt and uncle as well. He'd drop her off at her home in his Dodge Charger and then go have sex with some other woman he knew. He told me all of this in Spanish and I understood it.

The only thing I couldn't understand then or now was how he expected that information to make me feel better.

MURAKAMI, HARUKI. *SOUTH OF THE BORDER, WEST OF THE SUN.* PRINT.

"I almost drowned in the ocean yesterday—I probably shouldn't have tried to swim after five margaritas. I didn't want to tell you and mommy, though." I tell my dad this as we watch the waves crash on the shore of the resort in Puerto Vallarta during breakfast. We both start laughing hysterically. He calls me a cabrona who should take it easy on the chupe. He didn't want to come to Puerto Vallarta. He wanted to stay in his pueblo, but my mom and I begged and pleaded and there we were—three magical days of laughter, sol, and sipping "Miami Vices" and "Changos Sucios" by the pool. After breakfast, we walk on the beach together, my mom still asleep in the suite. He asks if I remember when I was a little girl and we would pick seashells together at the Rosarito Beach Hotel. My mom and sister still asleep, he and I would wake up at dawn and find the best shells on the beach. I look out at the Pacific and smile. Shell-collecting with my sapo is one of my favorite memories and I'm glad my dad in his seventieth year remembers, too. "The Rosarito Beach Hotel is where I *learned* how to swim," I say. And this is the last time I will ever stand on a beach with my daddy. If heaven is a real place, I imagine my sapo will be waiting for me on the shore, handing me the best bottle of tequila that heaven's cantina has to offer and ready to help me pick sand dollars off the ground.

LOW LATTITUDE LUST

In a mixing tin, combine:
1 shot Vodka
1 shot Southern Comfort
1 shot Cherry Juice
14 oz. Pineapple Juice
Shake well and pour into a brandy snifter.

I am 9, 10, 11, 12, 13, 14, 15, 16, 17, 18, 19, 20, 21, 22, 23, 24 years old and my mommy says she can touch it because she made it.

She is referring to your A-cup breasts. When she was nine years old, her uncle touched her newly formed A-cups breasts every night. The child of a mother who may (or may not) have ridden away on a horse[119] never to return, and a father who also abandoned her,[120] your mother was raised for a few years by three aunts and an uncle in Guadalajara. None of the aunts ever noticed when the uncle would cross the threshold of her room late at night and touch her little breasts. When your mother becomes a mother, she is more "handsy" than most, yes, but it is never malicious, never mean, never lustful—she just doesn't understand what boundaries are.[121] She will simply come into your room—sometimes when you're changing or reading or watching television. She will sit on your bed and grab them, either over or under your clothes. Sometimes, she'll laugh. Sometimes she will use it as an opportunity to give you advice: If a man that you don't like grabs them, you should tell someone. And if a man you do like grabs them, make sure you love him before you let him go any lower.

....

[119] *See also* **"Woolf, Virginia."**

[120] *Also sip* **"Trailer Wench."**

[121] Because your mother doesn't understand what boundaries are, perhaps that is also why *you* struggle with boundaries too. For more on this topic, *sip* **"Batida Abacaxi."**

NABOKOV, VLADIMIR VLADIMIROVICH. *LOLITA.* PRINT.

In my teens, I thought I had a thing for dirty old men,[122] but after all the older gentlemen in coffee shops that have approached me over the years (hoping to get one last taste of the young stuff), I've had it. Somewhere between the one who tried to give me a sensual foot massage in a Coffee Bean to the 65-year-old one—who called me his Little Princessa, stalked me at a Starbucks in Beverly Hills, and offered to take me on a trip to Ensenada—dirty old men have lost their appeal. I just wish I could read a book in peace without the Humbert Humberts of the world trying to get a piece of my "Lo. Lee. Ta."

. . . .

[122] *See also* **"Bukowski, Charles."**

BEND OVER SHIRLEY

In a Collins glass with cubed Ice,
Add:
1½ oz. Raspberry Vodka
4 oz. Sprite Soda
¾ oz. Rose's Grenadine Syrup
Stir and garnish with 1 Muddled Cherry

I am 20 years old and ask the comedian/screenwriter/production designer[123] to spank me on the musty carpet of his San Fernando Valley apartment. His hand might as well have been a paddle cactus across my butt cheek because it brought tears to my eyes. No one has spanked me that hard before or since. I've asked many men, but no one[124] has been able to bring it above a playful tap.[125]

---

[123] *See also* **"Fitzgerald, F. Scott"** and **"Rhys, Jean."**

[124] Actually, The Editor, twelve years your senior, did a pretty good job.

[125] For more cocktails that can make you shout, *pair also with* **"Screaming Pornstar."**

O'BRIEN, TIM. *THE THINGS THEY CARRIED.* PRINT.

"My parents came to this country with a few pesos in their pockets and a baby on their back." That is how the first line of my student's essay begins. That summer before law school, one my four jobs[126] was to teach first-generation high school students how to write their college entrance essays. The rest of the essay had the spirit of some of my papi's favorite rancheras. When I was little, rancheras were how I knew my papi was home from work. He would blast them out of his khaki-colored pickup with the windows down and they carried throughout that suburban neighborhood in California. When I rode with him in the truck, sometimes I tried to turn down the ballads about Guadalajara, to soften the heat in my chubby cheeks, but he only turned the music back up, and even louder. And I crouched down lower into the hot leather when he did. Now, I understand that the gritos issuing from the speaker—their painful tenderness—were his purest form of protest, at having to live in a neighborhood that wasn't built for him. It seems clear now. Now, as I myself blast my "Rancheras y Mariachi Essentials" apple-music playlist into my ears, as I take my seat in an Ivy League law classroom in New York City that wasn't built for me.

. . . .

[126] And even with four jobs, you are light years from breaking out of that first tax bracket.

ALL AMERICAN

Shake with Ice:
1 oz. Bourbon
1 oz. Southern Comfort
2 oz. Coca-Cola
Pour into All American glassware
and garnish with a Lemon twist.

I am 20 years old and my papi decides to become a U.S. Citizen after nearly four decades in the United States.

Your mami became one in 1994, the second she could, but your papi has been in permanent-resident land for years. Maybe he thought he would be living back in Mexico[127] by now. Maybe he thought he wasn't smart enough, and that he didn't know enough English to take the test. Maybe he never wanted to learn enough English to take the test. But his family is in America and it is becoming difficult for LPRs to travel freely across the border. And he misses his Mexico lindo.
So, he studies, and your older brother helps him prepare, even accompanies him to the interview. Your older brother Nacho is handsome and a smooth talker—a natural car salesman, after all. Your brother convinces the woman conducting the interview to allow him to be in the room while your papi answers the questions. Your dad does phenomenally with the first few. And then the doozy at the end: "Who appoints the justices to the Supreme Court of the United States?"
Your brother winks at the woman and asks if she will let him translate that one. For your brother, anything. Your brother looks at your Dad and asks, "Quién es el mero mero?"
"Pues el presidente," your papi replies.
"Wait, did he just say the PRESIDENT?" the woman exclaims.
"He's a citizen!" Your dad is ushered out of the office in a whirl of affirmative paperwork—a citizen but not quite understanding what exactly just happened.

. . . .

[127] *See also* **"Dickens, Charles."**

ORWELL, GEORGE. *NINETEEN EIGHTY-FOUR.* PRINT.

"I like him because he's not a politician," the white woman on the trolley in Old Town Alexandria says on my second date with The Editor. All that doublespeak and he still finds fans. The Editor suggests we hop off at the next stop and we do. Earlier, The Editor took me to a vineyard, then we walked his dog and I told him how my students were working on a project undercutting the Mexicans-are-rapists-and-murderers rhetoric, and then we had sex for the first time, an hour after that. Over a year later, in Manhattan, I am reading *Plessy v. Ferguson* for ConLaw and watching the electoral map on my computer screen start to fill in. I tell The Editor I am going to sleep but that I am scared. He tells me not to worry, but he's white and part of the media, so he doesn't entirely get it. I wake up at 2am to a text from The Editor that reads, "It's not over. But it's not looking good."

1815

2 oz. Razamazzotti Amaro
½ oz. Lemon Juice
½ oz. Lime Juice
1 oz. Ginger Ale
Garnish with a round of Cucumber
and a slice of Ginger.

I am 15 years old and in AP European History class, the day I learn the year Napoleon was defeated at Waterloo.

That was also the day your father yelled at you when you rolled your eyes after he told you to wash the blender.[128] You were a teenager and eye rolling came naturally, but your Dad was stressed because of work and the new white chef who was moving into his territory, so he found the eye rolling disrespectful.[129] That was the first time your Dad really yelled at you and cast you out of his kingdom for three months.[130] You both have that notorious stubbornness the Zapata side of the family is known for, so he stops picking you up from school and you walk home with your head high, especially when you see his pickup truck pass you by on the street. But then his sister, your Tía Sofia, dies in her kitchen of an aneurysm with the sink water still running. You and your father sit next to each other in the iglesia in Inglewood and when the mariachi starts playing, "Más állá del sol," you hold hands and cry together.[131]

[128] Generally, Mexican men don't appreciate when you roll your eyes at them. *Sip also* **"Adios Motherfucker."**

[129] For other things your father finds disrespectful, *see* **"Lawrence, D.H."**

[130] For the second time, *sip* **"Black and Blue Señorita."**

[131] For more mariachi, *also see* **"Allende, Isabel."**

PLATH, SYLVIA. THE BELL JAR. PRINT.

I read this book on the roof overlooking the backyard the summer after I graduated from college. Like Esther, I also saw my life branching out before me, unable to decide on a fig.[132] I couldn't find a job or an internship that summer, so my parents let me move back in and I watched *Mad Men* episodes in my pajamas all day and my Dad made me turkey sandwiches or fancy grilled cheese for lunch, always bringing them directly to my bed. My parents had rented out my sister's old room that year for some extra money and they asked me to clean it out. The previous female tenant had left behind a DVD under the bed—*Strap-On Girls Volume 17*. I ended up watching some of it after I finished all the episodes of *Mad Men*.[133]

....

[132] *See also* "**Cisneros, Sandra.**"

[133] *Pair also with* "**Screaming Pornstar.**"

ELECTRIC FUZZY

In a Collins glass, combine:
1 part Peach Schnapps
2 Parts Lemonade
Stir with a pink swizzle stick.
Drink until everything is blurred.

I am 21 years old and my college roommates and I spend hours browsing at a sex shop in Culver City.

You forget how it started but it might be because all four of you attend a college with a crucifix in every classroom, a sacred chapel as the campus's focal point, and classmates who are largely still virgins. And so, whenever anyone is bored or wants to procrastinate on their paper or movie script, you all hop in your car and peruse the aisles—lube, porno parodies, cock rings, lace lingerie, vibrators. While other roommates may go to the mall and end up leaving with the same style of sweater, you all buy the same model of vibrator, the "Lucid Dream," in different colors. Whenever the thought of post-grad weighs heavy and comes sharply into focus, you love turning it on between classes to feel everything whirl into fuzz.

PROUST, MARCEL. *IN SEARCH OF LOST TIME.* PRINT.

Whenever I dip pan dulce in oil-patched milk straight from the cow, every morsel brings me back to the spring I spent at my Tía Eva's in Aguascalientes.

It is near the end of my third-grade spring break that my mom's sister Eva recommends they take me to a clinic to see about my mouth-breathing problem. The Mexican doctor suggests I get my tonsils and something in my nose removed; so my mom leaves me in Aguascalientes for the operation and returns to California for work. I spend weeks and weeks at my Tía Eva's, healing from my surgery. There, I am expected to communicate with everyone in Spanish and avoid the room in the back of the house where they keep my uncle's sister, who is a little "enferma de la cabeza," they all say. Finally healed, my Tía Eva puts me on an Aeroméxico flight in a pretty dress and a large hat, like the kind Rose wears in *Titanic.* My family picks me up at LAX and takes me to Red Lobster for my homecoming dinner. Returning back to school late, I need to catch up on all the lessons I missed, and almost don't make it into the fourth grade. In fact, my mom has to re-enroll me in elementary school because word around the playground is I have moved to Mexico.

NOCHE DE PHOOF

1 oz. Vodka
1 oz. Light Rum
1 oz. Crown Royal
2 oz. Pineapple Juice
Shake vigorously with Ice
until its frothy on top.

I am 26 years old and scream words so loud in Spanish during sex with a white-man-of Irish-descent: "Ay qué rico. Dámelo papi. Más duro. Necesito tu verga."

You'll have done it on every inch of his Woodley Park apartment, leaving marks on every wall you meet. When you both catch your breath, he'll turn to you and tell you he wants to talk to you about the Spanish. If you're doing it to impress him or make him feel good, you don't need to. In fact, he'd prefer it if you didn't scream things in Spanish at all. English will be just fine.
You'll turn to him, push back his sweaty and matted ash-blonde hair, and tell him: "I didn't do it for you. I did it for me."

QUEIRÓS, EÇA DE. *COUSIN BAZILIO / O PRIMO BASÍLIO.* PRINT.

The Teaching Assistant sends me messages in Portuguese and I send him messages in Spanish and somehow we understand. As first- and second-years in our graduate program, and as writers, our messages are filled with subtext layered underneath subtext. Still, I'm trying to save my over-analyzing for my seminar papers. Besides, I have a long-distance boyfriend. Still, one day, The Teaching Assistant has a love song—written by a Mexican and sung by a Cape Verdean—playing in the graduate lounge, at an hour I know he knows I'll be there. That's when I want look into his big blue eyes and tell him: "Quiero mirarme en tus ojos." He's the petrichor I've been waiting for, but he has a girlfriend he loves who moved all way from Korea, where they had both taught English, to be with him. And I like her a lot. The Teaching Assistant is a large part of why I finally break up with my boyfriend back in Los Angeles for good.[134] If there's someone I want more, why would I settle? I want to tell The Teaching Assistant that, but I don't want to lose him, and I don't want to lose her, so I sign up for an online dating site for the first time and hope, with time, I can see him as a brother, or at least as a cousin.

....

[134] *See also* **"Ernest, Hemingway."**

BATIDA ABACAXI

Shake with Ice:
2 oz. Cachaça
4 oz. Pineapple (fresh), chunks
½ tsp. Granulated Sugar
Strain into Collins glass and Stir in 1 cup Crushed Ice.

I am 25 years old and my roommate says Portuguese sounds like someone put Spanish into a blender.

That's the year you feel not just caught in a love triangle but caught *between:* your current boyfriend; your second-year love interest ("The Teaching Assistant"); his fiancée; and the married red-haired girl—you feel trapped in a love tesseract. That summer, you will have to teach alongside The Teaching Assistant . He'll have just graduated from the program and you'll be moving into the second year. You'll have to hide it from your students, how you are suffering from a breakup with your long-distance ex-boyfriend, and on top of that you are working with someone your heart longs for but can't have. In law school you'll still be friends with The Teaching Assistant and his fiancée until the night you get blackout drunk. Somewhere between discussing their upcoming wedding and getting a third pitcher of margaritas, you grab her breasts repeatedly, over and under her bra, at a bar on U Street. She will send you an email the next day telling you this, telling you that you crossed boundaries and that she is angry and hurt by what you did. There is no justification or excuse, you know, for replicating the violence done to you on the body of another woman of color if that's what you did. You're just incredibly sorry and want to tell her that—but you're sure she thinks you're complete garbage by that point and she wouldn't be wrong if she did. She makes it clear never to message, call, email, or text her again. She doesn't say it outright, but you also take her email to mean: you can never call, email, or text her fiancée, The Teaching Assistant , ever again. You promise yourself you never will, and hope they live a beautiful life together. You'll feel a pinch of cosmic loneliness when you make that promise.

RAND, AYN. *ATLAS SHRUGGED*. PRINT.

The man from the fancy firm, wearing the newly dry-cleaned
pinstripe suit, asks me what my favorite class was during 1L.
I want to tell him, *it was all hell,* but end up saying: "It's a tie
between Gender Justice and Property," and then I launch into
discussing Gender Justice, first. He stops me, sighs, and then he
shrugs. He tells me that I have a lot of immigration and gender-
related items on my CV but he needs to tell the law firm I can do
something else also, if I'm hired: "So, tell me about Contracts." I
remind him: "I said Property." "Tell me about Property then." In
the eleventh hotel room I've been in that day somewhere above
Times Square, I immediately launch into my most impressive
property law knowledge in my most annoyed voice. I want to tell
him, instead, that I've learned how to appear in court this past
summer, I learned how to write a brief, how to speak to clients
(in Spanish at that)—so even though it was in an "immigration"
context, it still translates. But instead, I shake his hand, take his
card, and smile when he tells me that I'll be hearing back from
the firm soon.

AMERICAN DREAM

¼ oz. Kahlua
¼ oz. Amaretto
¼ oz. Frangelico
¼ oz. Dark Crème de Cacao
Chill with Ice. Strain into a shot glass.

I am 27 years old and tell my mom I have 28 twenty-minute interviews lined up that week.

"I hope I at least get one offer for a summer associate job," I explain to her. "That would mean $3,500 a week for at least 10 weeks next summer. She tells me she's sure I'll get one because she's been praying to the Virgen de Guadalupe. I tell her that my boyfriend, The Editor, took me to the outlet mall that weekend so I could buy four different suits. I bought most of them from JC Penney, and a fancy Calvin Klein one from the Bloomingdales outlet, along with a black leather portfolio for the resume copies I'll print on linen paper. My mom tells me she's proud of me and my dad comes on the phone and reminds me that when my mom was a little girl, she was covered in dirt and swam in a river full of leeches. And when he was a little boy, all his family ate was beans three times a day. My mom comes back on the phone and tells me she's so happy with all that I've accomplished, and how I still keep reaching for the stars.

When I'm about to hang up she reminds me to smile and wear my high heels to the interviews.

RHYS, JEAN. *WIDE SARGASSO SEA.* PRINT.

I'm home for Christmas vacation and I finish the final chapter
of this novel sitting on a rock at Castaic Lake where my parents
would take me to picnic when I was a little girl. That night I
dream I leave my parents' house in the suburbs behind and sneak
my flask into The Comedian's comedy show in Hollywood. The
stage is bright and beautiful. The curtains are a deep-crimson,
roped in gold. The whiskey burns my throat but I still heckle him
from the back. With jokes like these, he makes it easy: I've never
been to Europe, but if I ever go, I have a feeling Berlin will really
take my breath away. He once had an angel in the sheets and
now he has a madwoman in his laugh factory.[135]

---

[135] For more on this "comic tycoon," *see also* **"Fitzgerald, F. Scott"** and **"Melville, Herman"** or even **"Thoreau, Henry David."**

FEEL THE BURN

Pour into a glass, neat, not chilled:
½ oz. Kahlua
½ oz. Bailey's Irish Cream
½ oz. Ouzo
½ oz. Wild Turkey
Light with a match.

I am 26 years old and I have my first physical examination in a long time, thanks to Obama and my newfound DC Healthlink.

The doctor tells you everything looks excellent and you put your pretty dress back on. But when you come back out, the nurse tells you to head to the doctor's office down the hall. "There's been some oversight," the doctor states, "You have chlamydia." You had never really wanted to admit it before but when "*see* 'Adios Motherfucker'" would fuck you, it sometimes *did* feel like he was popping a jalapeño pepper into your pussy. But when you asked him if he was clean, he yelled at you for an hour. "I'm not fucking dirty," he roared. You knew he was bad news, with the huge scar on his left arm where his ex-girlfriend Alondra had bitten off his flesh when he refused to let her jump out of the car mid-fight on the 101 freeway. It was so deep that he needed stitches. And yet, you stayed. And even though you broke up with him seven months ago and haven't seen him since—he's still fucking you. And because you're sleeping with two people now, you have to put your big-girl chonies on and tell them both.[136]

. . . .

[136] *See also* **"Stevenson, Robert Louis."**

ROTH, PHILIP. *PORTNOY'S COMPLAINT.* PRINT.

So, a few days after Christmas you cheat on your first boyfriend with a Jewish guy and now what are you going to do? Technically, it wasn't cheating. You and Pablo were on a break, you'll say. You don't love subscribing to cultural clichés but, really, as the Jewish guy always reminds you, he is an accountant who works on the same floor where you work in Beverly Hills, and he absolutely loves his mother. She's in town visiting and sleeping downstairs when you and the Jewish guy, after all the months of flirting in hallways, decide to take it there. Your first boyfriend was Mexican but no one in your family was crazy about him and you break up with him for good the next day. Your brother's second wife always said she pictured you with a Jewish man anyway, but the accountant in question doesn't picture himself with you. After three screws he breaks it to you, a few weeks into the New Year, but doesn't give you a clear reason. Weeks later you'll go drink with your best friend Cynthia in Hollywood, and when you come out of a Cuban speakeasy you see a Latin-Jewish-fusion food truck called "El Nosh." You'll sit on the curb in a lacy mini dress and cry into your yucca latkes covered in mango crema, with tourists walking by who just don't understand.

MOTHER'S MILK

In a cocktail shaker, mix:
½ oz. Bailey's Irish Cream
½ oz. Butterscotch Schnapps
½ oz. Goldschlager
Double strain into a handmade Rocks glass.
Top with Chicory Pecan Bitters.
Garnish with Coffee Grounds.

I am 5, 6, 7, 8 and I wish Martha #1 or Martha #2 were my real mommies.

They sleep in my room and hold me when I have a nightmare. They have me say my nightly prayers en español. They give me baths and wipe all the dirt from the playground off my skin with smiles and soapy loofahs. All my mom does when she gets home from work is yell. I learn from an aunt that my mom didn't even breastfeed me much. I sipped formula from a nanny because my mom returned to work at her beauty salon almost immediately after she gave birth to me. And for years, she'll point at the c-section scar, the one she said she had to get because I was stubborn even in the womb and refused to come out. She'll point and say, "You did this to me." She'll tell me that for years.

And it won't be until I'm a saucy teenager and walk into her walk-in closet—where she's gazing at the scar while running her fingers over the ridges—that I'll tell her: "Well, you should have told him "no" that night.

ROY, ARUNDHATI. *THE GOD OF SMALL THINGS.* PRINT.

My father compromised: he gave America nearly 75 percent of his life—fifty or so of his years, according to the death certificate, but Mexico would get his eternity.[137] My mom had purchased them "His and Her" funeral plots in Santa Clarita many years ago, but my papi never wanted an afterlife with a view of the 14 Palmdale/Lancaster Freeway and the barren fire-damaged hill behind it. When the unspeakable happens, my father's ashes are set to remain in my brother's house until December, when my family usually visits the pueblo in Mexico. But my mother calls us all and begs that we need to take him *now*. He can't rest if we don't take him now. As if the funeral in June weren't still fresh in our minds, we take our father's remains to Mexico at the beginning of September. I fly from New York City and meet my family in Guadalajara, sleep-deprived from all my layovers. We have another Mass for my father in Tenamaxtlán, this time in the church of my confirmation.[138] After the Mass, my family and all who loved my father in that pueblo, walk his ashes to the campo santo. Before we return to America, my brother, his girlfriend, his son, my mother, my sister, and I visit the grave for one last, painful adiós. Because it's the rainy season, the clay-like lodo clings to the bottom of our shoes. We all start kicking at the cement with the underside of our feet outside the campo santo's gates, six people looking as if they are doing the Mexican hat dance on a Sunday afternoon.

. . . .

[137] *See also* **"Dickens, Charles."**

[138] *See* **"Irving, John"** for the first Mass.

ALEBRIJE

Gather and shake:
½ oz. Vodka (Bacardi)
½ oz. Rum
½ oz. Amaretto
Strain into a chilled Coupe glass.
Garnish with Fennel Pollen and Raspberry Dust.

I am almost 29 years old when we entomb my father's ashes during the harvest season in Jalisco.

The previous Christmas vacation in Mexico, you spent many mornings petting your uncle's horse, El General, in the corral after breakfast. In the corral he was gentle and sweet; during the corridas in the evenings at the bullfighting stadium, he was fierce and strong. You always knew your father's sign was Sagittarius—fitting for the wild horse galloping inside of him that often trampled on the civilized. In your father's eulogy, you wrote: *Ignacio era como los caballos que el adoraba—fuerte en la pista de carrerras que fue su vida, siempre echándole ganas pero tambien cariñoso con la gente que el amaba.* The day after he's entombed, you come to the campo santo by yourself, sipping tequila from a red plastic cup. You stare at the grave he shares with his parents, next to your great-grand parents, Juan and Bernarda. As you stand facing the generations a heavy rain will start to pour down and you imagine a magnificent horse made of dazzling fuchsias, lime-greens, and electric yellows snorting sweetly at your back—sent to guide your daddy into the next life.[139]

. . . .

[139] For more on horses, *see also* **"McCarthy, Cormac"** and **"Shaffer, Peter"** or *sip* **"Horse and Jockey."**

RUSHDIE, SALMAN. *MIDNIGHT'S CHILDREN.* PRINT.

At the strike of noon, my older sister slammed the sliding van door on my forehead with all her weight, after unloading the groceries, after she had forgotten to unload me first. My sister Karina said she didn't know I was still in the van and didn't anticipate my little, wobbly, toddler exit. Still, years later—after my mother tells us she once walked in on my sister yelling into my crib, telling me that she wished I had never been born because she was no longer the favorite—I'll tease her and say that she must have really had it out for me in those early years. There's a picture of me with an engorged forehead and scars on my nose, and horror stories of an emergency room visit. Because of this accident, to my mother I'll become the most unappealing "mouth breather" in the years to come, and she'll take me to every ENT in Los Angeles County. At parties, in front of everyone, she'll tell me to breathe through my nose, even though I just can't. Later, in my teens, a doctor will defend me to my mother, saying that even though my mother may not like how it looks, I can breathe and that's what matters. I'll stop having to go to ENTs around then. In the end, my sister will say this accident is the reason why I turned out so smart and I'm a real Mexi-*can*. It's because she knocked some sense into me.

NOSE CANDY

In a shot glass, combine:
¾ oz. Tequila
¼ oz. Tabasco Sauce
Garnish with Powdered Sugar.

I am 21 years old, it's New Year's Eve, and our entire house smells of garlic that carries upstairs and clings to all our clothes.

My Dad has started a small catering company to make extra money, and he cooks the food in our kitchen, but also on the industrial-strength appliances he has hooked up in the garage.

That was always the thing about my dad cooking versus my mother. My mother could cook a meal for 5 and the mess in the kitchen looked like she cooked for 500; my dad could cook a meal for 500 and the kitchen would look like he cooked for 5, at most. It took my mom years to convince him to start this business and now she's trying to convince him to charge more than $10 per plate. "It's five-star food," my mom tells him. "They don't need to know where it was cooked." But that's precisely my dad's concern. I leave them while they discuss this to attend a party at my old friend Brooke's.[140] My clothes smelling of garlic, I'll be so engrossed in catching up with her that I'll miss my best friend, Cynthia, trying to tell me that all these people are coming out of Brooke's tiny bathroom in Pasadena like it's a clown car. *And* they keep rubbing the skin underneath their noses.

. . . .

[140] Yes, we remained friends years later despite **"Henry, James"** because she gained weight in college and realized she was merely mortal like the rest of us.

SALINGER, J.D. CATCHER IN THE RYE. PRINT.

While drinking with friends in Los Angeles, one friend is visiting from college and tells us about all the trippy "East Coast Types" she's met while living in places like Baltimore and New York City. She tells us the Holden Caulfields of the world are real. The fancy prep schools are real. And people have honestly asked her questions like, "Where do you summer?" We all laugh our SoCal laugh. Where do I summer? When I move to the East coast, I'll see them all for myself. One day in law school I'll even be blindsided by girls in my ConLaw review session bragging about each of their respective prep schools. The fact that I went to a public high school in California, a really good one, will have no place in their conversation. That's also around the time I honestly consider dropping out of law school, after I found out I didn't get a cushy firm job for my 1L summer and don't know how I'll be able to finance my rent for 2L without taking out more loans. I'll tell my mom this. She'll tell me she's thought about it, and she'll delay her retirement for a year and send me the money from her social security checks. I cry. "I'm supposed to be taking care of you by now, Mom," I tell her between tears.

She tells me: "I'll always take care of you, as long as I still can."

MANHATTAN BELLA

Shake and Strain:
2½ oz. Bourbon (Knob Creek)
⅜ oz. Dubonnet Rouge
⅜ oz. Sweet Vermouth
2 Dashes Angostura Bitters
Pour into a Martini glass.
Garnish with a Brandied Cherry.

I am 26 years old and leave Washington, DC at 2am so I can make it to Manhattan before sunrise.

You haven't really driven a vehicle since moving from Los Angeles to DC two years ago, and so, you don't really want to share the road with too many other drivers. While you used to be able to put salsa on a burrito and steer with your knees through the Hollywood Hills, DC transportation has made you soft and you are no longer the driver you once were. The rental car is packed, half with things you brought from Los Angeles, the other half knick-knacks you accumulated in the District. You didn't sleep much before you left and are running on fumes: two large Monster Java drinks and slaps to the face every 30 miles. You concentrate on the road and avoid fiddling with the radio for fear you might crash if you do. That means you are forced to listen to a pop radio station you wouldn't have listened to otherwise. When you see the Manhattan Skyline and are listening to an extra sugary voice singing about staring at the blank page before you, you'll prepare yourself for the Lincoln Tunnel.

SHAFFER, PETER. *EQUUS.* PRINT.

We had so much "swag" from Hollywood Park in our house growing up that I almost feel like I was raised in cult of horse worshippers, and I am really surprised I haven't blinded six horses with a steel spike myself. Towels, backpacks, keychains, figurines, beer cozies, shot glasses. You name it. On select Sundays, my mother did try to make a day of it and spend time with her family at the racetrack, if that's where her husband was going to be anyway. In kindergarten, I love going to Santa Anita Park and spending the entire day on the swing sets arranged in the circle, where smiling children pumped their legs even harder for the chance to meet in the sky at the center with the mist from the fountain falling on us. And when my dad asks me to pick a number so he can place a bet on a horse, I'll feel important. And when I come back from a long day of swinging and he tells me the horse that I picked won, I'll jump up and down in a fit of glee.[141]

. . . .

[141] One day when you're older, you'll share this memory with your older brother Nacho, and he will laugh so hard. He'll tell you your father did this with all his kids, and no matter what number we picked, our father always told his children that the horse had won.

HORSE AND JOCKEY

In a mixing glass, half filled with Ice,
Stir and Combine:
1 oz. Anejo Rum
1 oz. Southern Comfort
½ oz. Sweet Vermouth
Add 2 dash(es) Bitters.

I am 5, 6, 7, 8, 9,10, 11, 12, 13, 14,15, 16, 17, 18, 19, 20, 21, 22, 23, 24, 25 years old and my mom asks me where my Papi is.

"I don't know." That's what you always tell her.

He uses his notorious catch phrase before he leaves. "Voy a verlas porque ellas no vienen." With his subtle smirk, he tells you he's off to see some ladies, but you both know where he's really going. He takes you out to Red Lobster on Sundays when he wins. Every time you eat those cheddar bay biscuits and order the coconut shrimp, you can hear the "and away they go" and see hooves hit dirt.

On Mondays, your mother's day-off from work, she calls the bank to check the balance and cries at the kitchen table when she hangs up. She tells you she works like una burra and for what?

SHAKESPEARE, WILLIAM. *THE TEMPEST.* PRINT.

I lived on an isle full of noises: snippets from the telenovelas
issuing from the TV, words my parents spoke, phrases my
Mexican nanny would say. And my mother will never let me
forget the time I asked my nanny, Martha (#2), not to speak
to me in Spanish when my friends were in the house. "Only
English, please." Martha's back stiffened as she stirred beans on
the stove. My father had been driving her to adult ESL classes
in the evenings at the local junior high school, so Martha knew
some English. If you don't practice your Spanish, you'll lose it
and you can't practice it with esas güeras, she told me. I told her
I didn't care. The adults on my island spoke to me in Spanish and
I responded in English. This is why my brother Nacho always
affectionately referred to me as his little coconut—brown on the
outside and white on the inside.

ISLAND TOY

In a Tiki glass half-filled with Crushed Ice,
Combine and Stir:
1 oz. Spiced Rum
¼ oz. Peach Liqueur
4 oz. Pineapple Juice
¼ oz. Lime Juice
Garnish with a Banana Dolphin.
To make a Banana Dolphin, cut off the end of the banana.
Next, carefully cut through the stem of the banana to shape the dolphin's beak.
Then, insert Whole Cloves to create its eyes. Last, cut a "V" shape at the base of
the banana. Add 1 Cherry in its mouth and set Banana Dolphin on top of
the cocktail, its banana fins hanging over the rim.

I am 8 years old and I play with the white girls down the street.

"Tag. You're it." "Take out the Barbies. And the Beanie Babies." "Don't forget Roary. Or Bongo. They're our favorites." "Build us a tent in your living room. The fancy living room." "Use the extra soft blankets your mom brought back from Mexico." "Can we jump on your bed?" "Can we use your sister's boombox?" "Can we read her diary with that skull on it?" "Can we jump on her bed?" "Let's play fashion executives." "Laura and I will own the company and you can be our assistant." "Miss Clancy always says you have the nicest printing so you can take very extra important notes for us because we're very extra important fashion executives." "Pile up the fluffy pillows at the bottom of your stairs so we can jump on them."

"Let's play on your Nintendo 64." "I will be Princess Peach like always, Laura will be Mario, and you can be Toad or Yoshi. You love being Toad or Yoshi." "Get us something to drink from your Dad's bar." "Why is there a worm in this bottle?" "Do you have Squirt?" "Do you have Fanta?" "We're hungry." "Don't forget, we're your guests, so you have to serve us."

SHELLEY, MARY. *FRANKENSTEIN*. PRINT.

My sister infused a spark of being into the lifeless thing that
lay at her feet. That thing was me. That night, the car I was in
had flipped at least three times and landed back on its wheels,
all because those teenage boys wanted to race on a secluded
mountain road. When we escaped the wreckage, I cried and
told everyone I didn't want to be there when the cops came. I
wouldn't know how to explain it to my Mexican parents who
thought I was sleeping over at Laura's. Kimberley, who was in
the car that didn't flip, calls for one of her boy toys to pick me
up and take me home but she's a total bitch about it, and I call
her one—for the first time. Boy toy drops me off and when he
drives away, I collapse on my driveway, left side of my face in the
water trickling into the sewer. I call my sister, Karina. She and
her boyfriend Carlos pick me off the ground. "I could have died,"
is all I can say. I'll live like an outcast in high school after that.
Lunches alone in the library. Piles of AP homework all around
me as my only friends. Afterschool job at a fast-food chain. The
Creation's monologues will strike such a chord—I'll walk by
white girls who were once my friends and feel spurned, wretched,
lowly.

MISCARRIAGE

In a shot glass, add:
1 oz. Vodka
1 tbs. Cherry Juice
3 dashes Tabasco
Garnish with 1 Muddled Cherry.

I am 22 years old and I spend a few days with my older sister, Karina, as she recovers from her first miscarriage.

After her husband Carlos returns to work and drops their first-born off at the grandparent's, she cries with her head in my lap and tells me that she was covered in blood on the bathroom floor when the fireman came in to save her. I let her cry more and I scratch her head, moving my fingers through strand after strand. She mentions that the fireman was pretty "hot" which made it even worse that he found her that way, found her in blood, sweat, and *nasty* granny panties. I spoon her tenderly from behind, muffle my chuckles into the skin of her back before we burst out laughing together.[142]

----

[142] For more spooning, *also sip* **"Is That a Banana in Your Pocket?"**

SMITH, BETTY. *A TREE GROWS IN BROOKLYN.* PRINT.

In your smartest-looking pencil skirt and matching blazer, you sit down at the table in the Michelin-star restaurant in Midtown. You are sitting with three female attorneys from the corporate law firm where you spent the past ten weeks of the summer. The menu reads like a poem, lunch is over $150 person, and the edgy snowman sculpture outside in the garden refuses to melt in the July heat. The attorneys know your father passed away around Memorial Day and they congratulate you on making it through with an offer from the firm, though they empathize that it could not have been easy for you. They ask you what drew you to New York City. You steal a line from a hippie yoga instructor you once had in Los Angeles. In tree pose, the instructor said: "the pose doesn't start until you want to get out of it." You tell them New York forces you to "hold the pose, so to speak." Your life was stagnant in California. Yes, you miss your family in Los Angeles, and you have no family in Manhattan, but you appreciate a city that forces you to grow. "Fair enough," they say.

LONG ISLAND

Fill a cocktail shaker with Ice
Add:
¾ oz. Vodka
¾ oz. Gin
¾ oz. Rum
¾ oz. Tequila
1 oz. Triple Sec
2 oz. Sweet and Sour Mix
Cover, shake, and then pour into a Hurricane glass.
Garnish with plenty of Lemon slices. The more sour the better.

I am almost 29 years old, my dad is dead, and I am completely untethered.

How else can you explain meeting a complete stranger for sex in a Marriot in Westbury after only sharing words on a screen? He says he is a rich lawyer and wants to "mentor" you. He's "mentored" law students in the past, even got an NYU law student a position at a white shoe firm. Before meeting, you told him you already had an offer from a law firm and didn't need help. You just wanted to have a "nice" time is all. But the moment you knock on the door, you have a premonition it will be anything but. When you step in, you see he must be over 600 pounds. Because all the sexting said you would have sex with him, you try to kiss him, even let him suck your nipple. But you're drowning in the miasma of his strong cologne, and he didn't bring a condom, and you tell him that you just can't. R&B music playing cheaply in the air, you tell him your father died of a heart attack three months ago and you just can't. You put your dress back on and start apologizing profusely. He roars at you: "Who's going to pay for this hotel room? I bill $800 an hour and I left work early for this?" He reminds you he knows a "big shot" at your firm. In a thick Jersey accent reminiscent of Tony Soprano, he threatens to send your pictures and the sexts to the "big shot" and tells you, "good luck finding another job."

You start begging him not to but then your legs just decide to run top speed out the door, all the way back to the LIRR station. And the conductor will barely be able to punch your ticket, your hands are so shaky.

SMITH, ZADIE. *WHITE TEETH*. PRINT.

After that one summer when a dentist your papi drove you to
see in Tijuana threw some of his unsterilized tools into your lap,
you avoid dental work south of the border. You were desperate
then because you were fresh from college with no job and no job
prospects. Luckily, your papi had you covered. But when you start
making a little money, you prefer going to the dentist's office
across the street from work in Beverly Hills. It's the office where
they filmed *The Hangover: Part II* and you would rather do that
than drive four hours into Baja California with your parents, no
matter how much cheaper it is. Your parents never see it that way
though. They continue to make special trips to Tijuana or stop at
a dentist in small pueblos in Jalisco when they go for vacation.[143]
It is not unusual for you to hear your parents say things like "se
me cayeron los dientes" (which horrifies you, frankly) or for you
mother to tell you the cement placed between her back molars
is so uncomfortable and she can barely eat. One time, your mom
will even be so desperate that she will get dental work done in
some Mexican lady's garage in Oxnard. She'll get a bad infection
from whatever they did to her. You and your sister will then have
to confront her: "¿Qué estabas pensado, mami?"

. . . .

[143] For more on your parents' questionable trips to Tijuana, *sip* **"Black and Blue
Señorita."**

MILK TOOTH

In a shaker filled with Ice Cubes:
1 Shot Jack Daniels
¼ Shot Crème de Cacao
½ Shot Blackcurrant Cordial
2 Shots Sweet and Sour
Strain into an iced Collins glass
over 1 Shot Pineapple Juice.
Place shaker over glass and shake hard once up
and down. Remove shaker and enjoy the froth.

I am 6 years old and the new kid in my first-grade class trickles his little fingers seductively down the skin of my back and down the length of my new stars and stripes dress.

Because of your last name, you are always at the back of the alphabetically ordered line and because he's new in class and there's only two weeks left until summer, the teacher, Mrs. Fennett, simply sticks him behind you. That first day, you think it is a mistake. Maybe he didn't mean to. But you keep filing in line to go to the lunchroom, to recess, to assemblies and it won't stop. You don't like it. It's not like when Ryan Riley, your first first-grade crush, accidentally brushes against you with his freckles when he comes back to the desk you share. *That* you like. But this feels wrong. You tell the new kid you don't like it, and to please stop, but he won't listen. You consider telling Mrs. Fennett or the TA but you just keep it to yourself instead. You figure there's only a few days of school left anyways.

And on the last day of first grade, you will lose your first tooth—your first milk tooth.

SOPHOCLES. *OEDIPUS THE KING*. PRINT.

Your mom wakes you up from your nap and asks if you want to
see a psychic your Tía Concha told her about. You have nothing
else going on that Sunday now that college is over, so you agree.
The oracle at Delphi lives in a small, unassuming home in the
seaside suburb of Oxnard and only charges 10 bucks per reading.
Your mom goes first and asks the usual questions: "Is my mother
still alive? If so, where is she? Is there gold buried in the house
in Mexico? If so, where?" Psychics are always 50/50 on whether
your grandmother is still alive. In the past, one psychic even
told your mother and some of her siblings that their mother
was still alive and lived in a small home in Aguascalientes with
another woman. Your mom, aunts, and uncles knock on the
door of the house the psychic pointed them to, but the woman
who answers tells them she isn't Carmen, she isn't their mother
(*see also* "Woolf, Virginia"). When it's your turn, you ask the
psychic about all your pending PhD applications. You want to
study literature and become a professor, you tell her. "Tu serás
una profesora," she says, and quickly brushes that aside. It's
more pressing for her to tell you about all the men she sees in
your cards. "They're coming," she tells you. "You'll soon meet un
moreno simpático." And in a few weeks, when you get your PhD
program rejections, you'll think the psychic was full of shit.

MEXICAN HILLBILLY

Almost fill a boot-shaped beer mug with:
16 oz. Corona
Drop: 1 shot Jack Daniels
into the beer and drink. Rápido.

I am 22 years old and can't find a job after graduating from college, so I work as a seasonal sales associate at Macy's in North Hollywood.

There I meet and start dating a Mexican boy on Christmas Day who is a year younger than me and makes everyone around us laugh. He lives in Sylmar in an apartment where his mom and little sister sleep in the living room, his younger brother sleeps on the couch, a tenant lives in one bedroom and he, Pablo, lives in the other and pays his mom extra rent to for it. Pablo introduces me to his little sister Tiffany, a name I find peculiar for a little Mexican girl. He introduces me to his mother, and she has a mouth full of silver like many aunts and uncles in my family. Pablo prefers going to my house because it's bigger and there's less people, but my house has Roman Catholic rules so we just end up having sex in Pablo's garage a lot. Like my father, Pablo loves watching telenovelas and one night he begs me to stay and watch one with him. When I come out, my car has been towed from the space Pablo told me to park in. "Don't worry about it," he said. It'll be the first of many more roadblocks in this relationship.

STEINBECK, JOHN. *THE GRAPES OF WRATH.* PRINT.

When I was in elementary and middle school, my dad gathered us in our jalopy and we drove the 48 hours into México to spend the holidays.[144] In high school, however, my parents gave me the option to stay home at Christmastime. I would spend Christmas Eve and Christmas Day with my sister, her husband, and my sister's Chilean in-laws, but the rest of the time it was just me and the tree. I was reading this book at 16, that first Christmas they let me stay home alone. I had no friends, so I wasn't throwing any wild parties.[145] Instead I read *Grapes of Wrath* cover to cover. I finished the final chapter on the couch opposite a candle with the Virgen de Guadalupe burning in the fireplace (my Dad always keeps a candle of the Virgen de Guadalupe burning in the fireplace). The final image of Rose of Sharon in the barn hit me. Hard. I thought about it when I packed up the nativity scene in the living room before my parents came back. After the holidays, my high school English teacher asked the class what we thought the ending signified. I said it was how I envisioned ideal motherhood to be, being so selfless and realizing that there's something bigger and wider out there other than yourself.[146]

. . . .

[144] *See also* **"Chaucer, Geoffrey."**

[145] *See also* **"Shelley, Mary."**

[146] Or, maybe, it's really just Steinbeck working through his Madonna-whore complex.

THE BLOOD OF SATAN

Layer into a shot glass
in the following order:
1 oz. Bailey's Irish Cream
½ oz. Goldschläger
1 oz. Jack Daniels
½ oz. Jägermeister
Gulp until you're in paradise lost.

I am 14 years old and attend my first rock concert at The Palladium on Sunset Boulevard. It's a Bad Religion concert. An older man with a greasy Satan tattoo on his torso keeps following my friends and I around the mosh pit with his pelvis.

You feel his penis bucking into your polka dots. He grabs you aggressively by the hips while the sound from the stereos throbs and pulsates. He harnesses your gyrations to the music for himself before you even know if you like it or want it. When you get back home to the suburbs, you and your friends compare notes. You later learn in a psychology course that what he does to us is called "frotteurism."

This was the first prick you had the displeasure of feeling. For another prick you had the displeasure of feeling, *see also* "Dostoevsky, Fyodor."

STEVENSON, ROBERT LOUIS. *THE STRANGE CASE OF DR. JEKYLL AND MR. HYDE.* PRINT.

Choosing between two eligible bachelors had started out like a Jane Austen novel but then morphed into *Dr. Jekyll and Hyde*. Even though you told them both that you were dating each of them, and would make a decision in your own time, moving between them begins to take its toll and even gives you déjà vu. On Super Bowl Sunday you'll wake up in a bed with one Virginia Gentleman[147] and then get your pussy licked that night in the bed of another Virginia Gentleman.[148] You won't remember which team won that weekend, but you'll feel like the winner, so it won't matter. Still, it will become difficult to balance both sets of piercing blue eyes, both map shower curtains, and the fact that they both work in offices in Rosslyn, and the copy of *Between the World and Me* they both have on their respective bedside tables, and when one of them wakes you up at 3am, commands you to stick your ass up into the air, pulls your hair into a ponytail and makes you watch yourself get fucked hard in the mirror above his bed, you won't even recognize *yourself* anymore.[149]

. . . .

[147] *See also* **"Brontë, Charlotte."**

[148] *See also* **"Kundera, Milan."**

[149] And when you find out your brother-in-law Carlos cheated on your sister, you'll think of these times. You'll think of all *your* half-truths. But you could barely juggle two men for two months, so juggling a wife, two kids, and a mistress for four years sounds plain evil to you.

WILD THING #2

*Add to blender:
Juice of 1 Lemon
Juice of 1 Lime
Juice of 1 Orange
1½ oz. Vodka or Rum or Tequila
1 Splash of Rosewater
4 tbsp of sugar
Blend until slushy. Pour into salt-rimmed Margarita glass.*

I am 27 years old and I meet the girl who turns me into a 14-year-old boy at the bar where she works in Georgia.

Raven-haired with cannoli curls rolled and pinned back with a red rose, she moves back and forth behind the bar in her black shorts, black corset, and black thigh highs. She looks like a the wildest of wild things. My boyfriend, The Editor, asks me to order him a "Bulleitt & Blenheim's" while he goes to the bathroom. And when my pin-up dream girl comes to ask me what I want, so playfully—I freeze. I look around at the bar, a place for playful adults in a college town, with all its mismatched tables and sofas. I'll manage to spit out that I want two Bulleit & Blenheim's . . . but pronounce "Blenheim's" wrong—I only realize when she hands them back to me. Then my boyfriend returns and gives me hot-and-fresh popcorn he picked up at the machine near the back—my boyfriend and dream girl start chatting but—like double Dutch in elementary school—I'm not sure when to jump in—so I don't. My boyfriend laughs at me because I'm not acting like myself around her.

On our tour of the South, I'll come back to this bar twice more. The next time, my dream girl is just getting off her shift. And the last time, the only bartenders working are friendly male losers that I have no problem talking to.

STOKER, BRAM. *DRACULA.* PRINT.

You're at a college retreat when your roommate slices up her future husband with a razor blade on the hotel bed.[150] He slices her back. You push him aside and lick the blood inching down her arm but not before you say, "I'll do it. I watch more vampire shows than you, Brad." When you get back to campus, Brad has to go to the hospital and get stitches, the cuts are so deep. He'll lie to campus police about how he got them and start dating your roommate after that, move out of his ex-fiancée's, and move in with you all for a bit. This Philosophy-Theater-combo, Brad, wears no shoes around campus and tells you not to be a lawyer. He says you all can just live on a commune after you graduate and be artists together.

You'll lose touch with them after college but reconnect again your first year of law school. You'll stand on their balcony, which has a sparkly view of Manhattan, and Brad will tell you about his first few months working at Covington & Burling, then shrug his shoulders and say, "Yeah, we're basically yuppies now."

. . . .

[150] Make sure to *sip* **"Summer Mind Eraser"** for more.

ETHNIC SUGAR

Mix in a Hurricane glass with Ice and stir:
5 oz. Cointreau
4 oz. Coca-Cola
2 oz. Tequila (Jose Cuervo)
1 tsp. Kool-Aid
Then fill with Surge Citrus Soda.

I am 5 years old and see my mother slap my sister, her own flesh and blood, across her face after we come home from buying groceries at Price Club.

There, my sister had photos developed from a disposable camera. Many were of her and her Latino friends in the quad in high school looking like a Delia*s catalog but one of the photos was of her kissing her boyfriend, Marcos. Marcos was a boy who lived across the "other" railroad tracks in the part of Santa Clarita everyone called "Little TJ." His family was from Zacatecas and he was dark and my mom didn't like him. This was one of many boyfriends my sister had to "fight" for, including Carlos, her future husband. My sister always told us she didn't want someone handsome like my brother and father. She didn't want someone stuck-up and sangrón. They'll just "cheat" on you. She wanted someone kind and it didn't matter what they looked like.

Still, my mom made her disapproval very clear—on my sister's face. This was probably another reason I didn't have a boyfriend until my 20s.[151]

. . . .

[151] *See also* **"Bukowski, Charles"** *and* **"Márquez, Gabriel García."**

TAN, AMY. *THE JOY LUCK CLUB.* PRINT.

She calls herself the rare hybrid: Colombian mother who gave her sweet Spanish and Chinese father who gave her mooncakes. You thought you had left her behind in Washington, DC for good,[152] or that she would move back to New Mexico, where the son she had as a teenager lives with his grandmother and great-grandmother. And yet, you hear through the grapevine that she'll be moving to NYC to start an MFA program at the same time you're starting your second year of law school. You know the city is smaller than people think, and you are sure you're bound to run into her at some poetry reading or museum event. The friends you kept in the "divorce" mock her choice of program, but your concern is more for her son who she's already been away from for three years, and now will be an additional two. You wonder if she should be there in New Mexico, instead of allowing her mother, grandmother, and her ex's family to raise him while she walks the streets of New York. But you're not a mother and you do not have her backstory, so you push your opinions to the side.

. . . .

[152] *See also* **"Díaz, Junot."**

CHINA WHITE

Pour into a shaker filled with Ice:
½ oz. Irish Crème
½ oz. White Crème de Cacao
Strain into white ceramic shot glass.

I am 17 years old and my mom agrees to babysit my brother's son William that afternoon; and yet, I'm the one left alone with the red-in-the-face crying baby.

William wants his mommy and so do you. Your mother said she needed to go to the store and would be back in five minutes but there you are two hours later crying on the driveway with William who is also crying. You're there hoping your mom, or his mom will soon pull into the driveway, not only because you don't know what you're doing but also because you have so much homework. As you try to bounce him up and down and kiss his cheeks through the storm of tears coming out of his eyes, you remember a time you and your mother were yelling at a decibel close to William's. You were 13; your mom said something about your nose and the hair above your lip that hurt you and escalated, and your sister had to intervene. You ran to your room in tears but still heard your mom scream in English, "I never had a mother—maybe I don't know how to *be* a mother!"

You remember this and think, as you hold William, *If she doesn't know, how am I supposed to?* [153]

---

[153] For more on your mother's mother, *see also* **"Woolf, Virgnia"** and for more on motherhood, *see* **"Salinger, J.D."** *or sip* **"Mother's Milk."**

THACKERAY, WILLIAM MAKEPEACE. *VANITY FAIR.* PRINT

I come home from a slumber party at a friend's where I've been watching horror films all night to find a real horror show: my mom throwing a permanent-makeup party at our house. Tired from a sleepless night, and unaware my mother would be hosting family and her close friends, I am completely blindsided by beloved tías with freshly tattooed eyebrows and my godmother walking around the kitchen with deeply etched eyeliner. My mother opts for permanent lip liner that puffs up her lips for a few days. And whenever she tells us to do something for her that week, it is hard for my older sister Karina and me to take her seriously with those Mick Jaggersized labios. We'd fall to the tile in a fit of laughter and my mom would beg us to stop making fun of her.

FRENCH COSMOPOLITAN

Add to a shaker with Ice and shake until chilled:
1 oz. Absolut Citron
½ oz. Grand Marnier
½ oz. Sweet and Sour
½ oz. Cranberry Juice
Garnish with a Lime twist.

I am 13 years old and ask my mom to sign a permission slip so I can start taking French classes at the high school, even though I am still in middle school.

Your friends were always talking about France, and you thought it sounded charming. You thought it would be no problem—you were always asking your mom to sign forms or permission slips and she rarely asked any questions. But that day she does and she rips the permission slip in half. "You are not learning French when you can't even speak Spanish," she screams. "You'll take Spanish next year and you'll do what I say."

Your uncles already call you a pocha, and poke fun at you for not knowing certain palabras so you think she has a point. The next year, you sign up for Spanish to fulfill the language requirement—but "Spanish 1" and not "Spanish for Spanish Speakers" because you'd rather be in a room outpacing the white kids than feel ashamed in a room surrounded by Latinos.[154]

....

[154] For more on the battle to retain your language and heritage, *see also* "**O'Brien, Tim**" or "**Shakespeare, William.**"

THOMPSON, HUNTER S. *FEAR AND LOATHING IN LAS VEGAS*. PRINT

When your parents married in 1974 they honeymooned in
Las Vegas and have been honeymooning there ever since. Your
first time in Vegas was in 1994 when you were in kindergarten,
and you remember your mom handing you a sausage biscuit
in a parking lot with a castle named "Excalibur" behind her;
you remember walking on the yellow brick road at MGM and
finding scarecrow; and you remember watching a pirate battle at
Treasure Island (and the De Niro voiceover from *Casino*, about
how the city was advertised as a family friendly place in the
1990s, will ring so true for you one day). You remember scary
men yelling at you if you talked too long to your mom when she
sat at the slot machines, and having to find your father in smoke-
filled auditoriums with horsies prancing on the screen. You
remember getting the news about Princess Diana's death while
sitting in a hotel room at Circus Circus. You've seen *Mystere* at
Treasure Island, *O* at the Bellagio, and *Love* at The Mirage. You
spent half your childhood in Vegas, it feels, and the funny thing
is that you've never returned to this desert mecca, with or without
them, after turning 21.

DESERT WATER

Add 1 oz. Tabasco Sauce
to the bottom of a shot glass, then fill with
1 oz. Tequila
Then drink 8 oz. water
(you really should be drinking 8 oz. water
after every drink but you forget, I know).

I am almost 19 years old and my parents take me to a casino on an Indian reservation near Solvang when I'm on summer vacation from college.

It's your first time gambling and your parents teach you how to sign up for free casino credits. You pick a desert-themed machine covered in coyotes and cacti. You put the card in and you're not too sure what to press. Your father comes over to see how you're doing. You touch some red button and then the cactus on top of the machine lights up and the coyotes start howling: you've won 300 bucks.[155]

You and your dad laugh together and hug, giddy with excitement. After, you eat at the seafood buffet and your dad orders you a beer. On the way back to Santa Clarita, a Linda Ronstadt song comes on the radio. You sing along in the backseat of the SUV: "pero si vieras como son lindas estas boracherras." Your parents are surprised you know the words and can sing it so well. "¿No que no soy Mexicana? Y Ándale."

. . . .

[155] The next summer, you bring a friend to this casino for her birthday, and you lose $100. That's the second and last time you have gambled and you're glad you're technically up $200 bucks. That's where you want to leave it.

THOREAU, HENRY DAVID. *WALDEN.* PRINT

The comedian/screenwriter/production designer told her they were going on an adventure. He told her to pick him up in San Fernando and not to ask any questions. They reached the desert at 3am and laid out her sleeping bag, bottom shelf whiskey soon splashing down their throats. In Joshua Tree, he brushed his skinny, pale fingers down her back. It was electric. Every segment of her spine vibrated. Her vagina, inches away, tingled. He pinned her to the desert floor and when she opened her eyes in between kisses, she saw the desert sky frame his disheveled hair. It was a sight she never could see in Los Angeles where the smog and the lights of tall buildings siphoned away the power from the celestial bodies in the night sky. Here, it was perfect. "I want you to fuck me," she said. Even though she hadn't seen him in months. Even though she had only done it once before.[156] Even though she was scared a rattlesnake was going to bite her in the bare ass. "I'm going to," he said. His Han Solo attitude was everything. And when they reached civilization in the morning, the angry voicemails from her mother screaming at her in Spanish about why she wasn't in her bed didn't matter. All the girl wanted was to fall asleep again in the comedian/screenwriter/production designer's arms surrounded by dirt and earth, listening to the low desert hum and coyote howls.

. . . .

[156] *See also* **"Fitzgerald, F. Scott."**

HOT CREAMY BUSH

In an Irish coffee mug, combine:
1 shot Irish Whiskey (Bushmill's)
¾ Shot Bailey's Irish Cream
6 oz. Hot Coffee
Top with Whipped Cream
And 1 Maraschino Cherry.

I am 21 years old and I write: "in the San Fernando Valley, all roads somehow lead to liquor and labium."

Months before, I had ended up at XPosed, a strip club on Canoga, with the comedian/screenwriter/production designer and his friend. After experiencing a joint lap dance we could barely afford, The Comedian and I ran to the back seat of my car. I released a guttural cry when he was done but managed to spit out: "I hate that I love you." I could barely get my clothes back on when The Comedian's friend, and a stripper he found, opened the door and joined us in the backseat. "I was thinking we could make it a foursome," the friend said. The stripper's name was Jessica, and she deposited all her crumpled bills in the pouch behind my driver's seat. The Comedian needed a smoke but told me to have fun before shutting the door. Jessica said I was beautiful and so were my breasts. She tenderly took one areola and then the other into her mouth. Weaving my fingers into her scalp, holding her at my chest, and then bringing her in for a deep kiss, I began to float away until The Comedian's friend took out his erection.

I hopped out of my car to find The Comedian but all I could see was my Honda Civic pulsing violently and rhythmically up and down in the parking lot.

TOLSTOY, LEO. *ANNA KARENINA*. PRINT.

The professor tells you that "*Anna* is a love story but that love stories depend on things like matrimonial boredom and regret—a story about love is hardly ever about love," and you fall in love with that notion. He then turns to the passage about monogram towels in Faulkner's *A Rose for Emily*. "What has Emily prepared for?" he asks. Having undressed a fellow male student in your cerebral cinema for the first half of the class, you'll know *exactly* what Emily has done, and what she does every night with the corpse between her sheets. One of those rare moments you will raise your hand and speak: "For her wedding night. Basically, it's her honeymoon." The professor will nod and conclude the lecture with his theory that Faulkner's story is the most romantic story ever told. Emily has her perfect honeymoon every night, feels the cold embrace of the man she loves every night. The English-major-of-British-descent will smile at you. You know he's a Sagittarius like your father. To find out how our love story ends, *see* "Austen, Jane."

FREIGHT TRAIN

Pour into shot glass:
½ oz. Jack Daniels Whiskey
½ oz. Tequila.

I am 25 years old and I help a red-haired woman cheat in the bar bathroom while her Salvadoran husband sits in the Irish parlor room, waiting for us.

We're at some tavern on M Street and she and I kiss passionately, pinballing North, then South against the subway tiles, and then bouncing West, then East. She tells me we should stop and goes to wash her hands, but I come up behind her, move my hands to her waist, and slowly start to shimmy her jeans down to give her a few final kisses on her white cheeks. It's the era where we call each other "slick kitties from the city" after both having read it in Audre Lorde's *Zami*.[157]

Months later, she'll mean it when she tells me to stop. She'll apologize and say it's because her head hurts all the time, she's breaking out in hives, she's always out of breath, and blacking out in strange places like the G2 bus. Her therapist will recommend a psychiatrist who diagnoses her as bipolar and recommends she take lithium for the rest of her life.

. . . .

[157] *See* **"Lorde, Audre."**

TWAIN, MARK. ADVENTURES OF HUCKLEBERRY FINN. PRINT

You two were thick as thieves once,[158] almost like Huck and Jim on that raft but now, even though you've both moved to the same new city and are enrolled in the same Ivy League institution, you barely make eye contact on the streets, in the library, in grocery stores. You want to tell her that the racial costume she put on to get into her Comp Lit PhD is the ugliest one you've ever seen. That she's a liar and a thief for taking a "diversity" scholarship with the help of her new surname.[159] You'd rather jump into the river of Manhattan traffic than chat with her on the street—she notices and gives you the bitchiest "don't die" before you officially get the light. Seeing the white man against the black that's telling you to cross and the Seinfeld diner in the distance, you remember the time she fingered you beneath the table in a college tavern and smelled her fingers after. One. By. One. You smile because that's a memory that a married woman will always have to live with.

· ·

[158] *Sip* **"Silk Panties with Lace"** and *take another gulp of* **"Freight Train."**

[159] For more on white people and scholarships, *also sip* **"James the Second Comes First."**

FLAMING CONFEDERATE

In a shot glass, add:
1 Dash Grenadine
Then layer, ½ oz. Godiva liqueur
Then float, 1 Dash 151 Proof Rum (Bacardi)
Use lighter to ignite.
Blow out to imbibe.

I am 25 years old and my brother Nacho tells me that he beat a piñata shaped like Donald Trump with a bat and the video went viral.

He is the General Manager of a car dealership, and he took swings at it with a fellow employee in the parking lot of the dealership.
As a former Marine who likes counting his dollars, my brother has always been a Republican in a fiscal and military sense, but singling out Mexicans for being "rapists" and "murderers" is where he draws the line.

He tells me the video has been taken down but even so, for a whole week, he kept getting calls at work from people with Southern accents threatening to murder him for what he did to that piñata.

UNAMUNO, MIGUEL DE. *HOW TO MAKE A NOVEL / CÓMO SE HACE UNA NOVELLA.* PRINT.

These stories spring up like Hydra heads but that's what you wanted, writer and reader, isn't it? Some are harder to swallow than others, true, but here you are making your way through this shaken and stirred abecedarian. You, writer, have pored over and poured over cocktail apps on your iPhone 6, filling pages of potential concoctions you found during downtime working at a law firm. Sometimes, there's debate: would **"Bruja Mexicana"** or **"Witch's Tit"** pair better with **Arthur Miller**? Writer, **the long list of books** you've read in your lifetime has come in handy. You never wanted to believe that undergraduate professor when he said that in order to be a writer, you need to be a reader. You wanted to write and who had time to read? But here you are now. And you, reader, does this make you want to read more?

BOOKMAKER'S LUCK

Shake well in cocktail shaker:
1 oz. Absolut Vodka
1 oz. White Rum
½ oz. Orange Juice
Strain into Highball glass ⅓ filled with Ice Cubes
Add 2 oz. Ginger Ale
Pour ½ oz. Crème de Banane on top
Give it 1 stir and drink.

I am 4 years old and I like telling my mom stories when she's on the toilet—stories about witches and princesses and dragons.

"Who told you that story?" she asks.
"I made it up, mommy," I say.
She gets constipated a lot. "What's 'constipated'?" I ask.
"It means nothing will come out," she says.
And we can stay there for at least an hour and then she'll start telling me stories about being a little girl in Mexico. One time, the Coca-Cola company came to the rancho and she won a singing contest they had. She stood on top of a crate, belted out a song, and won Coke bottles for everyone. Even when I get older, I still sit with her, and she tells me other stories. Stories of having to live with three aunts and an uncle who would "hurt" her.

One day I'll also meet the three aunts who cared for her. They live in a labyrinth of chairs and newspapers in a crumbling house in Guadalajara and sit together sewing like the Fates on moth-ridden couches. One of their husbands is the guy who climbed on my mother when she slept, but he's passed away by that time.

My mom will flush, and then I'll make a note of her stories in my journal.[160]

....

[160] For other instances of Bookmaker's "luck," *also see* **"Shaffer, Peter"** and *sip* **"Horse and Jockey."**

VONNEGUT, KURT. *THE SIRENS OF TITAN.* PRINT.

Fourth grade and you're begging you mom for a Furby. You admit, they're kind of strange—like a gremlin or a creature from a different planet but the girls down the street have them. In fact, Laura Tyler has five. Her favorite (and your favorite) is her Statue of Liberty Furby. It's the little felt torch with the little fur flame you're after. But it costs $40 dollars, and your mom isn't too sure she can manage that this month, she tells you. But she ends up getting you a tiger-striped Furby the next month. You tell this story to The Editor, explaining how Laura ended up starring in a low-budget science fiction movie about an industrial worker in a dusty world who receives "enigmatic" alien intelligence. You and The Editor refer to her as "Low-Budget Laura" from then on, whenever memory resurfaces her, even if that was always the furthest from the truth.

ALIEN URINE SAMPLE

¾ oz. Midori Melon Liqueur
¾ oz. Peach Schnapps
¾ oz. Malibu Coconut Rum
¾ oz. Crème de Banane
2 oz Sweet and Sour mix
½ oz Blue Curacao
Add 1st 5 ingredients to a cocktail shaker with Ice.
Shake and strain into a pounder glass.
Float Blue Caracao on top of brilliant green base.

I am 21 years old and my dad tells me over the phone that his job is laying him off.

He works at the banquet hall of a California State University and even the University President has commented on how delicious his food is. He technically doesn't have the title of "chef" but he can cook better than most who went to culinary school and can cook any cuisine as if he is a native—Italian, Jamaican, Ecuadorian. Still, they're letting him go because they need a head chef who is able to use a computer and make the weekly food orders and that's not him.

He tells me in that voice. The voice of a man who has lived in the United States since the late 1960s and still doesn't feel like he belongs.[161]

. . . .

[161] *See also* **"Dickens, Charles."**

WALKER, ALICE. *THE COLOR PURPLE.* PRINT.

Isabella/Nacio was my first roommate in the District of Columbia. I found them on Craigslist and they are Black, nonbinary, queer, a nursing student, and from Los Angeles. They are the reason I realize how important nonbinary pronouns are, and learned how to call people by the names they prefer.

Nacio/Isabella liked both names together, as well as separately and alternating. While they were home for Christmas in LA, they sent themselves a package with "Isabella" and "Los Angeles" as the "return address," and "Nacio" and "DC" in the "shipping to" area.

With Isabella, I live in a charming little two-bedroom apartment built in the 1920s with dark wood floors and a living room that looks made for Shug and Miss Celie.

With Nacio, the radiator hisses like an Amazon jungle in the winter, and sometimes we have to clean up the dead mice (that our traps catch) using their spare sex gloves and screaming in a way the gloves' pack-vertising didn't intend.

I love when Nacio/Isabella's girlfriend Gabby comes to visit. Gabby is a Dominican girl who lives in Canada, after her family fled there. When Gabby visits, the apartment is a scene out of *The L Word*: candles, the smell of vegan brownies in the air, fresh flowers from Trader Joe's on every table, Sleater Kinney as the soundtrack to couch cuddles, and their sweet moans as my nightly lullaby.[162]

....

[162] Isabella/Nacio eventually will move back to Los Angeles to be near their parents, and you'll have to find a new roommate, which will also end so bittersweetly. *See* **"Díaz, Junot."**

SATIN SHEETS

1 oz. Kahlua
1 oz. Bailey's Irish Cream
1 oz. Chocolate Liqueur (Godiva)
Whole milk
Mix liqueurs in an Ice-filled Old-Fashioned glass
Add Whole Milk to fill, garnish with Shaved Chocolate.

I am 15 years old and I have my first real crush on a Filipino boy who is in all my high school AP courses.

But he has a crush on the tall buxom child star in your grade who was once in *ER* and in a movie with Geena Davis. You can't blame him. She's gorgeous, after all. You remember her from middle school where she played flag football on the team with all the popular girls (you, of course, were on the opposing team with the other freaks). She and he sit behind you in Spanish class. You thought she didn't know you until one day, after you give a presentation in class, she tells you she loves you and loved the presentation. She seems sincere.
"It's nice to have fans," you say.

The next year, you hear a rumor that he and she exchanged "v-cards" and you imagine it must have happened on crimson or lavender sheets. And you'll realize you're not sure whether you're more jealous of her or him.

WALLACE, DAVID FOSTER. *THE PALE KING.* PRINT.

In America, the soundtrack to your father's machismo plays on loop: that famous Vicente Fernandez song paired with photos on a flat screen—many of them of he and you. Photos of you in front of the White House. At your graduations. On the beach.[163] The loss holding you down like a paperweight, your body still can't help rocking left then right to the "llorar y llorar," teardrops falling every which way. The 90-year-old aunt your father always said would outlive him and did put it best: "He died like a king." He sat down on his favorite upholstered chair, the throne of his suburban living room, never to rise again.[164] By the time you bring him to Mexico months later, he has turned to ash, to be housed in a beige box with a gold cross. At the campo santo, your sister tries to play Vicente Fernandez on her iPhone as the beige box is lowered into the ground. Your mom starts to speak over the song halfway through, suggesting your brother's girlfriend play the song your father's friend wrote for him instead.[165] Looking into your sister's helpless, near defeated eyes, eyes that tell you she just wants to play a song for her father, I scold my mother the way my father would have: "Just let the song play, Doña Rosa."[166]

. . . .

[163] *See also* "**Murakami, Haruki.**"

[164] *See also* "**Cather, Willa.**"

[165] *Also sip* "**Working Man's Zinfandel.**"

[166] For more on Mariachi music and rancheras, *see also* "**Allende, Isabel**" and "**O'Brien, Tim**" or *sip* "**Desert Water**" and "**The Black Widow.**"

THE BLACK WIDOW

1 oz. Black Sambuca liqueur
1 oz. Absolut Citron Vodka
Shake ingredients with Ice
Strain into chilled Martini glass.

I am 8 years old and realize Mariachi music
is the most essential ingredient in my family's life.

Mariachi players play at every family party you host and every family party you attend. Trips to the supermarket are all the more epic with your mother belting out a Rocio Dúrcal or Pepe Aguilar song at the top of her lungs. Every Sunday, your family drives to East Los Angeles for tacos and live Mariachi players, a sombrero on your head and murals of Mexican town squares on the walls. Your papi will buy your mommy shots of tequila and she will go on stage and sing for the crowded restaurant. Applause will bring a smile to her face. The year you graduate college, Casa Torres, the place in San Fernando, becomes your parent's home away from home. And though your daddy won't admit it out loud, he loves when his wife gets on stage, looks him straight in the eye, and sings that she wants "a real man and not a clown." When she's done singing, your papi will tease her that she was off that night, even if they both know it was perfecto. But the year your mother becomes a widow, she won't be able to sing Mariachi music anymore. "Because I no longer have the love of my life to serenade," she will say.

WAUGH, EVELYN. *BRIDESHEAD REVISITED.* PRINT.

The Editor may have called you his "abo-gatita"—his little lawyer kitten—but his support really ends there. Though you may have fantasized about marrying him on a beach in Mexico one day after law school ends, you know he does not deserve you for his bride. In fact, law school is giving you the jargon to describe the relationship: it's assymetrical. You're always hopping on a bus in Midtown and traveling five to eight hours, at least once a month, to visit him in Washington, DC. He came to New York one time, and then gone were his promises to pack up his puppy and his life in DC and be with you in New York during 3L. You're rarely having sex these days and his penis is constantly out of commission.[167] He does not want to have a child and you do. You may love him and he may love you, but there are limits to his love. You move mountains; he can hardly nudge molehills. You met when you were a graduate student in DC, but now you're a second-year law student in New York City. Maybe you are thinking like a lawyer now. On a cold December 23rd in Old Town Alexandria, he and his border collie find you drunk and crying in the park behind his condo. I need more, you'll tell him. You'll end up soaking his couch in tears for two days because you both know he can't give what you need. On Christmas Day, he will drive you to National Airport so you can make your flight to Mexico to see your family. You'll thank him and will know it's over for good the second he pulls away from the curb. [168]

....

[167] For more on the bittersweet joys of not having sex with the man you envisioned marrying, *see also* "**Hardy, Thomas.**"

[168] For more on "**The Editor**" *see also* "**Chopin, Kate**" or "**Hurston, Zora Neale**" or "**Kundera, Milan**" or "**London, Jack.**" And *take a gulp of* "**Cold War.**"

MAIDEN HEAD

3 oz. Cherry Brandy
2 oz. Cherry 7-Up
2 oz. Royal Cherry Soda Snapple
Mix liquid ingredients with a stirring stick in a white wine glass
Top with Whipped Cream
and 1 Cherry.

I am 15 years old and my mommy tells me the first and only man she has ever been with is my daddy. "He tricked me," your mother will laugh. "He didn't want me know who he really was. And he has been difficult, but I have always loved him."

They first met when she was 10 and he was 15 on the streets of the pueblo of Tenamaxtlán. She was chubby, dirty, dark, and covered in lice (he says); he was on his way to America. At 21, he returned to the pueblo after getting his green card and found her again, the most beautiful 16-year-old girl working at the store in town, but he already had a girlfriend.

In November 1973, she is 21 and he is 26 and they meet at a dance in Santa Monica, a fundraiser for the town of Tenamaxtlán. Married in May 1974 in West Los Angeles, your parents wed after less than six months of courting. Finding each other again after crossing the border, your mom knew he was special on their first date walking on the beach in Santa Monica. They will end up being married for 44 years, until death does them part. So, your mom knows what she is talking about when she tells you in her hardcore Catholic way to wait for someone you really love. Your sister Karina certainly listened. She's only ever had sex with her husband, Carlos.

But when it comes to sex, you have your father's "wild horse" spirit[169] that drives you further and further away from your mother's and sister's saintliness.

....

[169] *Also sip* **"Alebrije."**

WHARTON, EDITH. *THE AGE OF INNOCENCE.* PRINT.

I'll have my first kiss as my naked body stews in the waters of my lost innocence. All my other friends had theirs in eighth grade or earlier but mine won't come until eleventh. All those months listening to Led Zeppelin and Beatles records in the dark with those senior boys our group of friends found. All those months without touching, led us all here: five boys and five girls in a hot tub in suburban backyard paradise. That was the weekend the Lithuanian boy I saw for years in Roman Catholic Mass on Sundays, but never talked to, had an open house. His parents had gone to an Eagles Concert in Irvine. To this day, I am unable to listen to "Hotel California" without thinking of the truth-or-dare game that set everything into motion that night.

SUMMER MIND ERASER

Fill a Champagne Flute glass with Ice.
Pour: 3 cl. Peach Schnapps
3 cl. Midori Melon Liqueur
Top with Champagne
Let drink settle for one minute.
Push long bar straw right to the bottom of the flute
Drink from the bottom up.
Very important: DO NOT STOP mid-drink.

I am 20 years old and accidentally participate in my first (and only) college orgy—or honors-program "harem" as my roommate prefers to spin it.

It was a 4-day retreat in Newport Beach before classes started for everyone in the "nerd program," including the incoming freshmen. The seniors pull rank and say they're getting the swanky hotel beds, and the freshman can have the cots. But the seniors rarely make it back to their beds. We're too busy having hotel parties and after parties and after-after parties. It's the first time in my life where partying feels like a chore by the third day. On the last night, the night I thought I'd call it in early, I end up at one of these after-after-after parties. I'm in a bed watching my roommate getting her neck sucked by a senior, her pussy fingered by a junior, and her thighs kissed by a sophomore. I join in by licking my roommate's breasts, rewarded with an intensified moan.[170]

. . . .

[170] For more tales from the after-after-after party, *see also* **"Stoker, Bram."** And these tales are only the natural, logical conclusion if you *also sip* **"Electric Fuzzy"** while you're at it.

WHITE, T.H. *THE ONCE AND FUTURE KING.* PRINT.

I once heard my mom tell this story to an aunt. My mom rarely
drinks, unless she's about to go onstage to belt out a mariachi
tune and takes a quick tequila shot, but she may have been
drinking. I hear her recount a time when she was 22 years old
and newly married. It's the mid 1970s and she and my father
live in West Los Angeles and even though she is seven months
pregnant with my older brother, Nacho, she is also in the process
of studying to become a cosmetologist—wigs, scissors, bottles of
hairspray littered on the furniture and floor. She hears a knock
at the door and finds a woman who tells her that my once-
and-future father is the father of this mystery woman's baby.
The woman says that if my father ever wants to see his baby, he
needs to come to the diner across the street at noon the next
day or else she'll disappear forever. When my dad comes home
from his factory shift, my mom, knowing what it means to be
raised without a father, pleads with him to go to the diner, but he
doesn't show. This is a half-sibling I'll never know, and he or she
or they live on in our family lore and in the days of yore.[171]

---

[171] For a story you're certain your mother doesn't know, which corroborates this
tale, *pair also with* **"Sexual Healing."**

WHITE MEXICAN

1 oz. Bailey's Irish Cream
1 oz. Vodka
2 oz. Horchata
Garnish with Ground Cinnamon.
Stir with Cinnamon Stick.

I am 11 years old and I am heading to Las Vegas in a Lincoln Navigator to see my half-brother David[172] marry a Midwest farmer's daughter at the Excalibur.

His future wife has blue eyes and has a baby bump under her wedding dress. They marry in a small chapel near a turret, and the night before we watch a jousting tournament at the hotel where I eat a turkey leg with my bare hands and cheer for the red knight. Years later, I'll find a picture of their three children of elementary-school age on *Facebook*, all of them with brown hair, creamy complexions, and blue eyes. I'll remember my mother also has a strain of "white Mexicans" on her side of the family. I'll think back to my 8th birthday party where my white childhood friends bounced up and down in the AstroJump surrounded by my loud family, the corn my dad had planted in the backyard that year, carne asada and beans, the Dalmation puppy I received as a present, and all the mariachi music. I'll introduce them to one of my cousins and after the party, the güeras will ask me, "Why isn't your cousin brown like you?"

. . . .

[172] *Also sip* **"Papa Doble."**

WILDE, OSCAR. *THE IMPORTANCE OF BEING EARNEST.* PRINT.

"The sunhat's from Bloomies," your older sister told all the girls as they poured her lemonade from the pitcher. New to the neighborhood, Karina had been invited over to a fashionable pool party with other teens and pre-teens next door at Jennifer Kelly's. Jennifer had a white father and a Bolivian mother named Rosa. Rosa, like your mother.

Karina comes home and tells you all she had an amazing time, forgetting she left the sunhat behind on the lounge chair. On Monday, at the middle school, the girls from the party bully her because the sunhat was actually from Mervyn's and not Bloomingdale's. The Rosas will talk it out (en español) but it won't matter. Jennifer and Karina will go on to high school and both will try out for the cheerleading squad. Jennifer will eventually become head cheerleader; Karina will find refuge in her large group of Latino friends during lunchtime.[173]

. . . .

[173] *Also sip* **"Ethnic Sugar."**

DIRTY MEXICAN LEMONADE

Pour: 4 oz Bandolero Vodka to
into jar full of Ice.
Add: 8 oz. Lemonade
Slide lemon and lime wheels in.
Save: 2 oz. Sprite
for last.

I am almost 3 years old and my family leaves our one-story in Panorama City behind and upgrades to the two-story cookie-cutter in Santa Clarita.

It's the last one "in stock" and my mom scoops it up, even if it's not her favorite color. It'll be a longer commute to her beauty salon in North Hollywood but for "a huge dollhouse like this," she'll make it work, even if she and my daddy can barely afford the mortgage. There's a home video of my 3rd birthday party at that house confirming there was no landscaping those first few months. For the only Mexicans in the neighborhood, we sure didn't have the green thumbs of great renown. And some cowardly neighbor reminds us of this with the anonymous letter of family legend we received in the mailbox. My mom has its words committed to memory until this day: "You are dirty Mexicans who need to get a lawn. Your front yard is a disgrace to the neighborhood. Go back to where you belong." [174]

My family eventually gets green, green grass and ends up living in that neighborhood for over twenty years, among some neighbors who chose to remain anonymous.

. . . .

[174] For more tales of what it's like to be brown in the white suburbs, *sip* **"Pink Beaner."**

WILLIAMS, TENNESSEE. *A STREETCAR NAMED DESIRE*. PRINT.

Freshman year of college, the Honors Program you're in gets tickets to the campus production of this play. And because you and your classmates are all awkward freshman navigating the big safe space of college, the "rape" scene—where Stanley comes out in what you all dub afterward as "red ninja rape pajamas"—is a little too much to watch together. But by senior year, more of you are comfortable with each other, which is why you're able to throw a "Tarts & Vicars" party in your apartment, no problem.[175] That night, you'll passionately kiss your roommate who is dressed as "Roxy" from Chicago in front of two Mormon missionaries and then cry in your bed over "*see* 'Fitzgerald, F. Scott'" with your other roommate, who is dressed as a Catholic schoolgirl, consoling you. When putting your outfit for the party together, you had gone to your sister's house to borrow something "sexy." Your sister hands you lingerie but it has your brother-in-law's cum stain on it. You take it off and tell her you'll find something of your own.[176]

....

[175] It had seemed like a good idea after watching *Bridget Jones's Diary* together one night.

[176] For more stories about cum, *sip* **"Bloated Bag of Monkey Spunk"** or **"Sunday Confession."**

CLIMAX

Shake well with Cracked Ice:
½ oz. Amaretto
½ oz. Crème de Banane
½ oz. Triple Sec
½ oz. Vodka
½ oz. White Crème de Cacao
1 oz. Light Cream
Strain and serve as you please.

I am 8 years old and I listen to 2 CDs in my sister Karina's room: the *Grease* soundtrack (the 20th-anniversary edition) and *Now That's What I Call Music! (NOW)*.

I've lost track of what number we are on now. Over fifty, I presume. That one was the first one. "Zoot Suit Riot." "Sex & Candy." "Barbie Girl." "Say You'll Be There." In order to avoid doing her Econ homework, my sister would tease my hair and I'd dance around her room. For the finale I loved jumping on her bed, pretending to be Danny Zucko in a leather T-bird jacket. Her bed, pretending to be a red 1948 Ford Super Deluxe.[177]

. . . .
[177] For more climaxes in/on cars, *see* **"Hawthorne, Nathaniel."**

WOOLF, VIRGINIA. *MRS DALLOWAY.* PRINT.

Doña Flores said she would buy the medicine herself. And with that, your abuela's life has always been shrouded in mystery. When you were a little girl, she was always just that black-and-white photo your tías had in their houses, the one that stared at you wherever you stood in the room and made you want to run. She was your middle name, the one that your mom legally changed when you were 1. She was the woman who either disappeared or died when your mom was 5 years old. She was the woman who had 16 children but only 12 survived.[178] When you get older, you ask more questions. She had migraines a lot and one day she rode away on a horse, some say. Others say she died, even though the older children never saw a body. She had married a man she didn't love who impregnated her at least once a year because he had money, even though she had loved another boy from el campo more. Her favorite song was "Collar de Perlas," one about a woman who wants to fashion a pearl necklace out of her tears.

You find the song on YouTube and listen to it, and for once you cry, imagining what it must have been like to be the abuela you've never known and briefly shared a name with.

....

[178] Having recently asked an aunt, the number is actually 18, but your mom always told you 16.

BAHAMA MAMA

Shake with Ice Cubes:
¼ oz. 151 Proof Rum
½ oz. Dark Rum
½ oz. Coconut Liqueur
¼ oz. Coffee Liqueur
4 oz. Pineapple Juice
½ oz. Lemon Juice
Pour in Tiki glass
Garnish with as many Maraschino Cherries as you can.

I am 6 years old and receive birthday and Christmas gifts from my "adopted" grandma Shirley. That was always how my "adopted" grandmother signed my cards in a sweet, sweet cursive.

My favorite gift was *The Lion King* lunch pail and matching outfit with Simba and Nala rolling in the African grass paired with some purple tribal-like shorts. I figured my mom told Adopted Grandma Shirley I loved *The Lion King*. I figured my mom told my Adopted Grandma Shirley a lot of things. My mom never had a mother I could visit or make cookies with or to buy me gifts I loved but didn't need. I figured my mom told Adopted Grandma Shirley this while my mom styled her hair in the beauty shop.

In a few years the gifts will stop, and a few years after that, I'll think it was so nice that an elderly white woman I never met heard my mother's sad story and sent a little Mexican girl she didn't know all those gifts.

WRIGHT, RICHARD. *NATIVE SON*. PRINT.

The secretary typed him up a new birth certificate and handed it to him. This was his ticket to America. It was the only way he could pretend to be his uncle's son and cross the border. His uncle once had a son with the same birthdate as him, only two years before. Changing that one single digit, switching out the "9" for a "7", only stayed with him for decades to come. As a teenager, he had gone to the office in Mexico with his uncle, and the secretary had been so accommodating and he got swept up in the moment. But now it's the 1970s, the 1980s, the 1990s, the 2000s and he's scared the immigration officials will knock on his door, lock him up and then take him back for what he has done.[179]

---

[179] For more on the importance of birth certificates, *see* **"Lorde, Audre."**

AMERICAN BEAUTY

Shake with Crushed Ice:
1 oz. Brandy
½ oz. Dry Vermouth
¼ oz. White Crème de Menthe
1 oz. Orange Juice
½ oz. Grenadine
½ oz. Freshly Squeezed Orange Juice
Strain into chilled Coupe glass.
Float Claret Red Wine on surface.
Garnish with red rose petal.

I am 16 years old and eating at an Outback Steakhouse with my parents. My Dad has gone to the bathroom and left the check for my mother to take care of.

She tells me she had a good week at the beauty salon she owns, her New York strip was so delicious, and the waiter was so nice so she'll leave a big tip. As she fishes bills out of her Bank of America bag, she starts to laugh and tells me a story she sometimes tells when the bill comes. When she was 17 and newly arrived in this country, her older brother Pedro would take her on a tour of Los Angeles and take her to restaurants. This was the time when she liked painting moles on her face. Beauty marks, she called them. She couldn't understand why her brother was leaving all that money behind on the table. When Pedro would stand and walk away, my mother would scoop the money into her pocket or purse. Today, my mother keeps laughing and leaves a little extra to make up for the past.

X, MALCOLM. *THE AUTOBIOGRAPHY OF MALCOM X.* PRINT.

You'll teach an excerpt of this, the part where he learned to read in his jail cell, to first-generation college students in graduate school. It'll be paired with an excerpt from Richard Rodriguez's *Hunger of Memory*, the part where a young Richard learned how to read because of, and in spite of, his parents. And whenever you think of Rodriguez, you think of your mentor, the one you admire and who suggested you read Arturo Islas' *The Rain God* for your capstone project. Because you see patterns, you know that Islas, a Latino scholar, went to undergraduate at Stanford and was one of the first Chicanos in the United States to earn a Ph.D. in English. Rodriguez, a Latin@ scholar, also went to Stanford for undergraduate. And your mentor, a Latinx scholar, went as well. While teaching, you'll remember how your essay about learning to read got you into Stanford for undergraduate, too, but your mom told you to take the full scholarship to "esa escuela Católica," right down the 405 instead. Your parents didn't understand what it meant to get into Stanford, but they understood money so you watch the Chinese girl and the Jewish boy in your senior high school class go instead and move North while you stay in L.A. because Latinas just can't go to school far from home, it seems.[180]

....

[180] **If prestige is what you're after, you'll still have the opportunity to take out over $300,000 in federal loans for an Ivy League law school so it's no worries, really.**

LATINX LOVE

1 oz. Cruzan Coconut Rum
1 oz. Cruzan Banana Rum
3 oz. Pineapple Juice
1 oz. X-Rated Fusion Liqueur
1 oz. Coco Lopez Cream of Coconut
1 oz. Raspberry Juice
1 oz. Cream
1 scoop Ice.
Blend until smooth.
Serve in Hurricane glass rimmed with Grenadine
and Coconut Shavings.

I am 26 years old and my part-time lover's husband, her Latin lover, is crying in my lap.

You've just come in from a dip in the Atlantic.[181] and you and he are still so drunk post-wedding, and are the only ones awake in the beach house. He looks at you with big, brown, puppy-dog eyes like he wants to tell you something. He speaks. He'll tell you his wife disappears a lot. That sometimes she gets so lost in her writing and her Latino studies books, he doesn't know where she goes. And when she disappears he just doesn't know how to talk to her. You know that so much of their marriage is complicated. Part of it is that he overstayed a tourist visa and their marriage helped him stay in the country. He'll start to cry a little and you'll feel guilty you've put your hands on his wife's hips and run your fingers along her tender cheeks.[182]

....

[181] *See* **"Chopin, Kate."**

[182] *Pair also with* **"Freight Train."**

YEATS, W.B. *THE COLLECTED POEMS OF W.B. YEATS.* PRINT.

You've been in the poetry seminar all year and, by some miracle, are in invited to a dinner for The Poet, the one who even got a Ta-Nehisi Coates shout-out when she was awarded University Professor. You're in the University President's special wood-paneled dining room with all the Jesuit wine and flair and are seated next to a man with a Foundation named after him. On your right is your mentor who makes a joke that it's just like the Gay Thanksgiving he goes to in Adams Morgan—they always sit the Latino people next to each other. You fumble with your silverware, take too many sips out of your water glass, fidget in your bamboo chair, and are unsure which fork to use for your salmon. The Man with the Foundation becomes interested in the fact that you are currently deciding between Berkeley and Columbia Law. He suggests Berkeley so you won't have to take out all those loans. He tells you he knew The Poet when she was younger and starving. The President and the Provost look tipsy in the corner, and the wife of the man sitting next to you looks concerned that a young Mexican girl is monopolizing her husband's attention. You make a note to take the menu with you as proof that you were there, but you'll only end up leaving it on your chair.

WILD IRISH ROSE

2 oz. Busker Blended Irish Whiskey
½ oz. fresh squeezed Lime (or Lemon) Juice
¼ oz Sugar syrup (2 parts sugar: 1 water)
1½ tsp. Grenadine/Pomegranate Syrup
Shake ingredients with Ice and strain into a chilled Coupe glass.
Top with Club Soda for a touch of sparkle.
Garnish with skewered Lemon Zest Twist
& Luxardo Maraschino Cherry.

I am 25 years old and drinking Four Roses bourbon whiskey at the end-of-the-semester party surrounded by poets.

On the first day of class, our professor had gathered us in her office. I was one of the fortunate ones who found a spot on the couch, knocking knees with a fellow student and the coffee table. Others found space on the floor, two shared the ottoman, and the others in the class opted for the folding chairs she kept in the corner.
The Poet gave us a sentence:
"She told him that she loved him."
She told us to put "only" somewhere in that sentence.
We went around the circle in a symphony of shifted meanings.
"*Only* she told him that she loved him."
"She told him *only* that she loved him."
"She told him that she loved him *only*."
"She *only* told him that she loved him."

By the semester's end, with the snow falling outside, you're still in a circle but drunk enough to talk about your father's gambling addiction in front of everyone, including The Poet you love but who makes you so nervous.
"You should write about it," The Poet says.
You giggle because you're drunk and you can hardly handle it when she is able to look at you and see you.
The Poet takes a sip of wine, pauses, and speaks again. "You need to write about it," she says.

ZOLA, EMILE. *GERMINAL*. PRINT.

In Mexico, my father is not my mother's husband. The house he bought my abuelitos with his Nebraska meat-packing wages will not vest in her. Or in us. Birth names don't register. Dates don't register. Birth parents don't register. The man she married in California on a day in May does not translate back to Mexico. My mother, my sister, and I let this sink in on a December day seated under the avocado tree of the house in Mexico. We sit opposite the tile fresco of the Virgen de Guadalupe in the courtyard. My mother tells us she is working on transferring the property to herself. It will take at least a year but my cousin Natalia, who works as a lawyer in Guadalajara, can make the transfer as if my father had simply sold the house to my mother. Mexican property law recognizes that hombres can simply disappear.

My mother starts to cry in my sister's arms. "We were going to spend tiempos aquí y tiempos allá," my mother will say. "Pero ya no se puede."

I close my eyes to her sobs and imagine the way the house was before the renovation my mom paid for: tías and tíos filling every spare bed; abuelo in his pancho; abuelita washing dishes; and my papi in his Stetson with his alligator boots clacking on the tile. I tell them I think I should become a dual citizen. It might be easier to keep the house in our family that way. When the words escape me, I hear a horse trotting in the direction of my father's remains at the campo santo, the Virgen de Guadalupe smirking in the afternoon sun.[183]

. . . .

[183] For more on the gathering of women in the face of religious idols, *see* "**Achebe, Chinua.**"

SEÑORITA SIN TIERRA

2 partes Mexicana (sí se puede)
2 partes California Sur
Un parte Distrito de Columbia
Un parte Manhattan
Pellizco(s) Ingenio Feroz
Pellizco(s) Soledad Profunda

ACKNOWLEDGEMENTS

First, I would like to thank Manuel Muñoz, a writer whose work I truly admire, and Texas Review Press for choosing this book from the pile when I had already counted myself out. I am especially grateful for Pete "PJ" Carlisle for seeing this book so clearly and nurturing its growth. And Karisma "Charlie" Tobin for care and attention during the publication process. Muchísimas gracias—I really can't thank you enough.

This book also would not have been possible without all the teachers, professors, and mentors who either taught me important lessons about literature or helped me think critically about the world we inhabit. Thank you especially to the following (in the order I met you): Mary Ellen Kearney, Beverly Ladd, Pete Pew, Sarah Maclay, Chuck Rosenthal, Jodi Finkel, Stephen Shepherd, Kelly Younger, Paul Harris, Gail Wronsky, Carolyn Forché, Ricardo Ortiz, Norma Tilden, Pamela Fox, Christopher Shinn, Elora Mukherjee, Kendall Thomas, and Kimberlé Crenshaw.

Thank you to all the kind souls and kindred spirits I have encountered on my path who have helped me become an empathetic human being and a better storyteller: Shannon Kirk, John James, Timothy Lawson, Baldemar Gonzalez, Stephanie Colorado, Renee Whyte, Lauren Bergelson, Katherine Kleinot, S.J. Tilden, Hannah Shapiro, Antonia Miller, Claudia Nelson and so many others, including all those I have lost touch with but never forget.

Thank you especially to John James, one of the only people with whom I felt comfortable sharing an earlier iteration of this book, and who provided thoughtful edits and kind encouragement.

Many thanks especially to Shannon Kirk for showing me that choosing between being a lawyer and a fiction writer is a false binary.

And to Michael Bryan Nowotarski for being the warm, gentle wave on my shore when life became the shipwreck of my plans. For bringing more defiant music into my life that will fuel me into the future. For loving me where I am. Muchas gracias, mi amor.

Muchas gracias most of all to mi familia, including Beto, Vanessa, Juan and Amalia. Thank you especially to my mother and father for your stories, your strength, and your resilience. And papi—thank you for telling me for years that you couldn't read and could barely sign your name on a piece of paper so that I could write you a book you could read from heaven (and I know you'll forgive todas las partes cochinas and will think they are funny).

SPECIAL THANKS TO ALL THE LITERATURE THAT MADE THIS BOOK POSSIBLE

Achebe, Chinua. *Things Fall Apart*. Penguin Classics, 2006.

Allende, Isabel. *The House of the Spirits*. 1st American ed. New York, A.A. Knopf, 1985.

Austen, Jane. *Pride and Prejudice*. Edited by Vivien Jones, Penguin Classics, 2003.

Beckett, Samuel. *Waiting for Godot*. Faber & Faber, 2006.

Brontë, Charlotte and Stevie Davies. *Jane Eyre*. London, Penguin Classics/Penguin Group, 2008.

Borges, Jorge Luis. *The Garden of Forking Paths*. Penguin Classics, 2018.

Bukowski, Charles. *Women*. HarperCollins Ecco, 2007.

Burgess, Anthony. *A Clockwork Orange*. Penguin Books, 2011.

Calvino, Italo. and William Weaver. *If on a winter's night a traveler*. New York, Knopf, 1993.

Carroll, Lewis. *Alice's Adventures in Wonderland*. Dover Publications, 1993.

Cather, Willa. *Death Comes for the Archbishop*. New York, The Modern library, 1931.

Cervantes, Miguel de. *Don Quixote*. Translated by P. A. Motteaux, Wordsworth Editions, 1992.

Chaucer, Geoffrey. *The Canterbury Tales*. Translated by Nevill Coghill, Penguin Classics, 2003.

Chopin, Kate. *The Awakening*. Penguin Classics, 2018.

Cisneros, Sandra. *The House on Mango Street*. Bloomsbury Publishing PLC, 2004.

Conrad, Joseph. *Heart of Darkness*. Eds. Robert Hampson and Owen Knowles, Penguin Classics, 2007.

Cooper, James Fenimore. *The Last of the Mohicans*. New York, Bantam, 1989.

Cortázar, Julio. *Hopscotch*. Pantheon Books, 1987

Danticat, Edwidge. *The Farming of Bones*. Abacus, 2000.

Defoe, Daniel. *Robinson Crusoe*. Penguin Classics, 2012.

Díaz, Junot. *This Is How You Lose Her*. New York, Riverhead Books, 2012.

Dick, Philip K. *Do Androids Dream of Electric Sheep?* Gateway, 2010.

Dickens, Charles. *A Tale of Two Cities.* Penguin Classics, 2012.

Dostoyevsky, Fyodor. *Crime And Punishment.* Signet Classics, 2001.

Eliot, George. *Middlemarch.* Wordsworth Editions, 1993.

Ellison, Ralph. *Invisible Man.* Penguin Books, 2014.

Esquivel, Laura. *Like Water for Chocolate.* Black Swan, 1993.

Eugenides, Jeffrey. *Middlesex.* New York, Farrar, Straus and Giroux, 2002.

Faulkner, William. *The Sound and the Fury.* Vintage Classics, 1995.

Fitzgerald, F. Scott 1896-1940. *Tender Is the Night.* New York, Scribner, 1962.

Flaubert, Gustave. *Madame Bovary.* Gallimard, 2001.

Forster, E. M. 1879-1970. *Howards End.* New York, Vintage Books, 1921.

Golding, William. *Lord of the Flies.* Faber & Faber, 2011.

Hansberry, Lorraine. *A Raisin in the Sun.* Random House, 1997.

Hardy, Thomas. *Tess of the D'Urbervilles.* Penguin Classics, 2012

Hawthorne, Nathaniel. *The Scarlet Letter.* Penguin Classics, 2015.

Heller, Joseph. *Catch-22.* New York, Knopf, 1995.

Hemingway, Ernest. *The Sun Also Rises.* Simon & Schuster, 2006.

Homer. *The Odyssey.* Translated by Robert Fagles, Viking, 1996.

Hurston, Zora Neale. *Their Eyes Were Watching God.* Virago Press, 2018.

Huxley, Aldous. *Brave New World.* 11th ed., Vintage, 2010.

Ibsen, Henrik. *A Doll's House.* Dover ed. New York, Dover Publications, 1992.

Irving, John. *A Prayer for Owen Meany.* HarperCollins, 2012.

Jackson, Shirley. *The Haunting of Hill House.* Penguin Classics, 2009.

James, Henry. *The Portrait of a Lady.* Penguin Classics, 2004.

Joyce, James. *A Portrait of the Artist as a Young Man.* Wordsworth Editions, 1992.

Kafka, Franz. *The Trial.* Schocken Books, 1999.

Kerouac, Jack. *On the Road.* Penguin Books, 2011.

Kundera, Milan. *The Unbearable Lightness of Being.* Trans.by Michael Henry Heim, Faber & Faber, 1999.

Lawrence, D. H. 1885-1930. *Sons and Lovers.* Toronto, Oxford University Press, 1913.

Lee, Harper. *To Kill a Mockingbird.* New York: Harper Perennial Modern Classics, 2006.

London, Jack and Brigit Viney. *White Fang.* Harlow, Pearson Education, 2000.

Lorde, Audre. Zami, *A New Spelling of My Name.* Crossing Press, 1982.

Martel, Yann. *Life of Pi.* Mary Glasgow Magazines, 2014.

Márquez, Gabriel García. *One Hundred Years of Solitude.* Trans. Gregory Rabassa, Penguin Classics, 2000.

Marx, Karl, and Friedrich Engels. *The Communist Manifesto.* Penguin Books, 2015.

Maugham, W. Somerset. *Of Human Bondage.* Csorna, Charles River Editors, 2018.

McCarthy, Cormac. *All the Pretty Horses*. Picador, 2009.

McCullers, Carson. *The Heart Is a Lonely Hunter*. Penguin Classics, 2000.

Melville, Herman. *Moby Dick, Or, The Whale*. Modern Library ed. New York, Modern Library, 1992.

Miller, Arthur. *The Crucible*. Penguin Classics, 2000.

Milton, John. *Paradise Lost*. Edited by John Leonard, Penguin Books, 2003.

Mitchell, Margaret. *Gone with the Wind*. Pan Books, 2014.

Morrison, Toni. *Beloved*. Vintage Classics, 2007.

Murakami, Haruki. *South of the Border, West of the Sun*. New York, A.A. Knopf, 1998.

Nabokov, Vladimir Vladimirovich. *Lolita*. 1st Vintage international ed. New York, Vintage, 1989.

O'Brien, Tim. *The Things They Carried*. Houghton Mifflin (Trade), 2009.

Orwell, George. *Nineteen Eighty-Four*. 1949. Penguin Classics, 2021.

Plath, Sylvia. *The Bell Jar*. Faber & Faber, 2005.

Proust, Marcel. *In Search of Lost Time*. Mumbai, Tingle Books, 2022.

Queirós, Eça de. *Cousin Bazilio*. Translated by Margaret Jull Costa, Dedalus European Classics, 2016.

Rand, Ayn. *Atlas Shrugged*. Penguin Classics, 2007.

Rhys, Jean. *Wide Sargasso Sea*. Penguin Books, 2011.

Roth, Philip. *Portnoy's Complaint*. New York, Random House, 1969.

Roy, Arundhati. *The God of Small Things*. Fourth Estate, 1997.

Rushdie, Salman. *Midnight's Children*. 1st American ed. New York, Knopf, 1981.

Salinger, J. D. *The Catcher in the Rye*. Little, Brown and Company, 1991.

Schaffer, Peter. *Equus*. New York: Scribner, 1973.

Shakespeare, William, et al. *The Tempest*. New York, Simon & Schuster Paperbacks, 2009.

Shelley, Mary. *Frankenstein*. Penguin Classics, 2012.

Smith, Betty. *A Tree Grows in Brooklyn*. Harper Perennial, 2005.

Smith, Zadie. *White Teeth*. Penguin Books, 2001.

Sophocles. *Three Theban Plays: Antigone; Oedipus the King; Oedipus at Colonus*. Trans. by Robert Fagles, Penguin Books, 1984.

Steinbeck, John. *The Grapes of Wrath*. Penguin Books, 2017.

Stevenson, Robert Louis. *Dr Jekyll and Mr Hyde*. Penguin Classics, 2012.

Stoker, Bram. *Dracula*. Wordsworth Editions, 1993.

Tan, Amy. *The Joy Luck Club*. Penguin Press, 2012.

Thackeray, William Makepeace. *Vanity Fair: A Novel Without a Hero*. New York, Modern Library,

Thompson, Hunter S. *Fear and Loathing in Las Vegas*. Harper Perennial, 2005.

Thoreau, Henry David. *Walden*. Pan Macmillan, 2016.

Tolstoy, Leo. *Anna Karenina*. Trans. Aylmer Maude and Louise Maude, Wordsworth Editions, 1995.

Twain, Mark. *The Adventures of Huckleberry Finn*. William Collins, 2010

Unamuno, Miguel de. "How to Make a Novel". *Selected Works of Miguel de Unamuno*, Volume 6: Novela/Nivola, edited by Anthony Kerrigan and Martin Nozick, Princeton University Press, 1976.

Vonnegut, Kurt. *The Sirens of Titan*. Dell Pub. Co., 1959.

Walker, Alice. *The Color Purple*. Wadsworth Publishing, 2006.

Wallace, David Foster. *The Pale King. Little*, Brown and Co., 2011.

Waugh, Evelyn. *Brideshead Revisited*. A.A. Knopf, 1993.

Wharton, Edith. *The Age of Innocence*. Wordsworth Editions, 1994.

White, T.H. *The Once and Future King*. New York: Ace Books, 1987.

Wilde, Oscar. *The Importance of Being Earnest*. Dover Publications, 1990.

Williams, Tennessee. *A Streetcar Named Desire*. Edited by E. Browne, Penguin Classics, 2009.

Woolf, Virginia. *Mrs Dalloway*. Penguin Books, 2020.

Wright, Richard Nathaniel. *Native Son*. HarperCollins, 2005.

X, Malcolm. *The Autobiography of Malcolm X*. Bantam Doubleday Dell Publishing Group, 1998.

Yeats, W. B. 1865-1939. *The Collected Poems of W. B. Yeats*. The Macmillan Company, 1977.

Zola, Emile. *Germinal*. Translated by Roger Pearson, Penguin Classics, 2004.